The O...

LEIGH DUNCAN

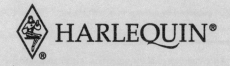

HARLEQUIN®

TORONTO • NEW YORK • LONDON
AMSTERDAM • PARIS • SYDNEY • HAMBURG
STOCKHOLM • ATHENS • TOKYO • MILAN • MADRID
PRAGUE • WARSAW • BUDAPEST • AUCKLAND

Recycling programs
for this product may
not exist in your area.

ISBN-13: 978-0-373-75308-6

THE OFFICER'S GIRL

Copyright © 2010 by Linda Duke Duncan.

This edition published by arrangement with Harlequin Books S.A.

For questions and comments about the quality of this book
please contact us at Customer_eCare@Harlequin.ca

® and TM are trademarks of the publisher. Trademarks indicated with
® are registered in the United States Patent and Trademark Office, the
Canadian Trade Marks Office and in other countries.

www.eHarlequin.com

Printed in U.S.A.

ABOUT THE AUTHOR

Award-winning author Leigh Duncan believes solid relationships lay the foundation for true happiness. Married to the love of her life and mother of two wonderful young adults, Leigh enjoys watching shuttle launches from her home on Central Florida's east coast. She writes the kind of books she loves to read, ones where home, family and community are key to the happy endings everyone deserves.

When she isn't busy working on her next book for Harlequin American Romance, Leigh loves nothing better than to curl up in her favorite chair with a cup of hot coffee and a great book. She invites readers to contact her at P.O. Box 410787, Rockledge, FL 32955, or to visit her online at www.leighduncan.com.

For Mom.
Your love of books inspired me to write.

Chapter One

The National Weather Service in Miami has issued
the following update: Hurricane Arlene will strength-
en over the next 24 hours. The storm is expected to
turn northward and avoid making landfall. However,
a hurricane watch remains in effect along the east
coast of Florida.

Stephanie Arlene Bryant killed her rental car's ignition and
emerged into the blanket of heat and humidity that passed
for late summer in Cocoa Beach.

"Just my luck," she muttered, hefting her laptop from
the backseat. "I've been in the state less than a week and
they've already named a hurricane after me."

Her mom would be so pleased. She'd always claimed
her youngest was the center of the universe. Having the
U.S. government weigh in would make it official. Though
there was a slim chance the folks back in Ohio hadn't
heard about the storm, Mom was sure to keep one eye on
CNN and one hand over her heart as long as her baby
lived in the Sunshine State. And with a hurricane off the
coast, spotty coverage was the only reason Stephanie's
cell phone didn't bleat like a lost lamb.

The quiet wouldn't last.

A quick glance at her BlackBerry confirmed the plethora of installations—phone, cable and Internet—scheduled by noon. By midday she'd be back to proving she was tough enough to make hard decisions and see them through. Space Tech had mandated a reorganization and streamlining of the Florida office, and sent her to make sure the job was done right. In exchange she'd been promoted to director of human resources. Her new position put her on the stairway to the CEO's office, but the job had risks. The kind that wrinkled her brow and made her wonder how soon was too soon for Botox. One slip in her twelve-month schedule, and she would tumble all the way down to the copy room.

Stephanie tucked an errant curl into place and blew a breath through pursed lips. She would never get another chance like this. She wasn't going to blow it.

Heels of her strappy sandals tapping like firecrackers, she pulled a freshly minted key from the pocket of her capris on her way up the pebbled walkway. Once inside the house Space Tech had provided for the coming year, she fumbled for an unfamiliar light switch.

"A beach house is supposed to be light and airy," she had told Deb, Space Tech's local Realtor, during Friday's walk-through. While the office was on the mainland, her bosses thought she'd enjoy living a short walk from the ocean. All new wiring and stainless-steel appliances made the older home the ideal spot for a rising corporate executive—but not if the windows were shuttered.

"They're just a precaution," Deb had answered with a shrug. "Hurricanes never make landfall in Cocoa Beach. It has something to do with the way the land juts out into the Atlantic. Storms 'swoop' on up the coast and out of our hair."

The woman had practically guaranteed the house was in a hurricane-free zone, providing a slew of maps and colorful brochures that hailed Central Florida's east coast as America's gateway to the stars and home to the world's second-busiest cruise port. And, since Stephanie's five-feet-two-inches wouldn't stretch far enough to take the panels down, Deb had agreed to have them removed.

Until that happened, thank goodness for air-conditioning and electric lights. Stephanie set a cup of coffee from a neighborhood convenience store atop one of the boxes the movers had stacked against a wall and began to unpack. According to her schedule, she should be settled in before the servicemen came and went. That would give her the evening to study personnel folders, a necessary task since she meant to have the names and faces of every Space Tech employee down cold before she reported to work in the morning.

But no one had showed by the time packing debris littered the house.

Convinced the installers would pull up to the curb the minute she headed for the closest pay phone, she felt compelled to stay where she was. She shoved aside a frisson of self-doubt along with a handful of rebellious curls. How she hoped to turn things around at Space Tech when her hair wouldn't even follow orders was a question she refused to consider.

The chin-length black ringlets were so not what she'd envisioned when she'd agreed to a corporate-ordered makeover. Neither were the sculpted nails with their pink polish. Or the closet full of frilly designer clothes. But the home office had ordered a softening of her usual buttoned-down and laced-up look, saying it was necessary to fit in with Florida's more relaxed culture. And since end results were all that mattered, she had gone along with the plan.

A plan that a few tardy workmen threatened to derail.

Stephanie threw the front door wide. Bright sunshine and summer heat streamed in, creating such a difference in the darkened and air-conditioned house that she stepped outside to soak up the warmth. A quick scan of the street provided no sign of a repairman—or anyone else for that matter—though she was just in time to see a flash of brake lights as a police car turned onto the next street. It seemed odd that no one was about on such a pretty day, but who knew? By the time her year in Florida was up, she might grow as bored as her neighbors with the scent of orange blossoms floating on soft ocean breezes. She gave the idea a shrug of disbelief and, propping the front door open, began to haul the empty, flattened packing boxes to the curb.

Monday, according to one of the brochures the Realtor had provided, was recycling day.

THE PULSING LIGHTS threw blue shadows across the hood of Brett Lincoln's cruiser as he drove past the boarded-up surf shops, bars and restaurants of Cocoa Beach. By now, most locals had fled the danger zone and only tourists lagged behind. But with the storm bearing down, even they were in a hurry to get out of town. The last thing Brett wanted was to get T-boned by some overanxious visitor so, even though it wasn't exactly regulation, he'd lit up the light bar.

Knowing the girls would love it was the extra bonus that put a smile on his face.

Brett gave the wheel a one-handed spin while letting Dispatch know where he could be found. Midway down Fifth Street, his smile turned into a full-fledged grin at the sight of a tall, wiry man trying to stuff an overweight chocolate Lab into the back of a minivan. It looked like a tight fit for a dog who obviously wanted no part of sitting among boxes of family treasures too precious to risk leaving behind.

"Need a hand?" Always eager to unfold his six-foot-four-inch frame from the confines of his police cruiser, Brett had the door open before the car finished rolling.

"Got four too many already," came the reply. "Here, Seminole."

All protests were instantly forgotten when Tom Jenkins pulled a rawhide strip from his pocket and let fly. The Lab executed a perfect midair catch, landing his tasty bribe in the van with the precision of an angler making the perfect cast. Tom gave the dog an affectionate ruffle before closing the hatch.

Brett crossed the postage-stamp yard in three long strides and shook the hand of the man he still considered his best friend, even if they didn't spend much time together anymore.

"Cutting it a little close, aren't you?" He pitched his voice low. Though the van's windows were up and the AC was running, the twins in the backseat had sharp ears.

"That's life for the self-employed." Tom shrugged. "Remember Dave Hartsong and Don Sinclair?"

"You mean Dan Hartsong and John Sinclair?" Brett asked with a smile. Tom could quote a boat's specifications down to the number of rod and cup holders, but he'd never get the owners' names right.

"Whatever. Those yahoos waited till the last minute to moor up. I'd have let them flounder, but they waved a fistful of money in my face."

Brett shrugged one shoulder in response. His friend would always be one of the last to cross the causeway linking Cocoa Beach to Merritt Island and the relative safety of the mainland beyond. To hurricane-proof businesses and homes took time and, if Hurricane Arlene hit them head-on, the exercise was apt to be futile. Yet everyone with any sense did it, and his pal was a smart guy. Brett's experienced gaze took in the heavy sheets of plywood covering the windows and all but one of the doors of the Jenkins' modest cement-block house.

"Where you headed?" he asked. Sturdy schools offered shelter in times of crisis, but none allowed pets. And it was too late to outrun the storm. Arlene would hit before sunrise.

"Finally found a kennel in Orlando to board Seminole. We'll stay nearby."

"The shelter on Lee Vista has openings," Brett offered. "I checked."

"Then that's where we'll be."

Brett would have said more, but at that moment a small woman wrestled two diaper bags through the still unprotected front door without stopping to catch the screen behind her. Wood slapped against wood. The noise echoed through the quiet neighborhood like a starting gun. In a sense, it was one. Tom bolted to his wife's side.

Brett didn't need to be all that intuitive to see that Mary was upset. The circumstances might warrant her tears, but hundreds of thousands of coastal residents were on the move, fleeing Hurricane Arlene's stubborn path and turning the sixty-mile asphalt ribbon to Orlando into a parking lot. Traffic would inch along for hours, and they all needed Mary to hold it together. He cleared his throat.

Tom shot him a warning look that made Brett reconsider the speech he'd planned. He nodded and spoke loud enough for all of them to hear.

"I'll check things out as soon as it's safe." Which meant the moment the wind stopped converting every loose palm frond into a lethal weapon. "She still has time to turn. Maybe the hurricane gods will smile on us this time."

"Let's hope so," Tom muttered. Shoulders slumping, he grabbed a hammer and moved away. Only two years before, a passing storm had all but destroyed his marina and his livelihood. Rebuilding had been both expensive and time-consuming. He couldn't afford to do it again.

"Hang on. I'll help," Brett said.

Even if he had known what else to say, words weren't necessary. Before he'd joined the force and his friend had met Mary, he and Tom had worked and played together so much they'd practically known each other's thoughts. It took only moments for them to wedge a precut slab of plywood over the front door. They hammered it and their frustrations into place with each nail.

"I'll call," Brett promised as he and Tom joined the rest of the family. "Let you know how it looks."

"Sounds like a plan," Tom answered. "Maybe it won't be so bad this time."

"Nah, couldn't be," Brett scoffed, keeping his thoughts to himself.

His pal had his priorities straight, and though Tom stood taller than before, Brett still detected the sour note of fear. Experience told him this was a good thing. Putting his family's safety first would keep his friend from doing something stupid—like staying on a barrier island through a Category 4 hurricane. Another handshake, this one lasting just a second or two longer than necessary, left Brett thankful they were both wearing dark sunglasses. He waited until Tom was behind the wheel to speak again.

"Stay right on my bumper till we get to the bridge. I'll peel off once you're in line to go across. Remember, that'll be the worst." In this traffic, crabs would make better time crossing the causeway than cars.

Tom, a veteran of more evacuations than anyone could remember, nodded. He knew the routine.

Mary's dark sunglasses were firmly anchored when she leaned forward. "You sure it's okay for you to do this?"

Getting a police escort from her husband's best friend was nothing new, but Mary always asked. Brett flashed a smile known to have an effect on women and got…nada. The expected response from his pal's wife left him feeling more unsettled than it usually did.

"Hey, we have to stick together." Brett shrugged. He took a long, careful look through the open driver's side window. Every required belt and buckle was securely snapped in place. He grinned at the identical two-year-olds in their matching car seats, one on either side of an enormous box of toys.

"Tell Mom who the good guys are," he said.

"We're the good guys!" shrill voices chorused in unison.

Brett gave the girls a thumbs-up and felt an unanticipated stab of envy when two chubby hands answered him in kind. Momentarily uncertain whether he was on the giving or receiving end of reassurance, he gripped Tom's shoulder in a final squeeze and was surprised to find his throat needed clearing before he was able to speak.

"Stay close," Brett growled before he headed across the sparse lawn to his patrol car where once more he hit the lights and siren. The girls—Tom's girls—loved it.

The brilliant summer sun had dropped several handspans and clouds gathered on the horizon before he saw his friends safely onto the causeway. Brett keyed his mike.

"Dispatch, this is Lincoln. Heading to Palm Royale to

resume the search for stragglers and anyone too bullheaded to leave when they're told."

Static crackled and spit until a soothing voice cooed through his earpiece.

"Just you wait, darlin'. A little longer and we'll have the whole town to ourselves. Won't we have us a time then."

Tension slipped from his shoulders as Doris, known to the officers of Cocoa Beach as The Voice of Dispatch, continued her patter. This time, Brett didn't have to fake the smile that formed on his lips. Doris, with her wiry gray hair and homespun ways, knew exactly how to defuse her "boys," as she called them.

"Can't wait," he returned. "Just you, me and what's-her-name."

"Arlene? That shameless hussy? She's just a big ol' puff of wind. You go on, now. Finish gettin' our citizens out of harm's way. Me an' the rest of the boys'll meet you at the station house. We'll all wait it out here where it's safe."

"Ten-four, Dispatch," Brett said before the patrol car's big engine roared to life.

He sped through neighborhoods of fifty-year-old squat, cement-block homes. Each was deserted and boarded up, the way it should be, and with all the traffic streaming onto the causeway behind him, he reached the end of his six-mile drive through Cocoa Beach in just over eight minutes. He slowed his patrol car to make a final turn, automatically noting each detail of the scene the way he had learned in the Marines and practiced every day of his four years on the force.

Something about the trim little house that sat practically in the shadow of the Palm Royale Condominiums prompted a second look, but nothing seemed out of the ordinary. After the storms the year before last, the Hensons had surprised him, choosing to replace the home's damaged roof and interior rather than razing the heavily damaged structure. The new white shutters and pale stucco reminded Brett of the Dreamsicles he used to buy as a kid when the ice cream truck rolled down his street on summer afternoons. He'd heard the house had recently changed hands and made a note to greet the new owners.

The radio crackled from the dashboard as if it were trying to remind him of jobs still unfinished.

With a shrug, he turned off Highway A1A toward the ocean. At the base of the towering condos, stately queen palms and manicured walkways separated row upon row of empty parking spaces. Like the little bungalow out front, the high-rise was buttoned up tight, as secure as it could be. Brett still hoped no one had left anything they *really* needed inside the half-million-dollar apartments. The building would be one of the first to face Hurricane Arlene's wrath. In a direct hit, she'd chew it up quicker than he could eat a piece of Kentucky Fried Chicken. Then, she would spit out the bones, leaving only a skeleton in her wake.

Brett shook his head and popped his seatbelt. There was nothing like impending disaster to make a man think too much.

The instant the driver's side door sprang open, the cruiser filled with a roar of surf that seemed far too loud beneath an increasingly clouded sky. Sand crunched under his shoes as he stepped onto brick pavers and took a deep breath. The air felt heavy and hot. A storm was coming all right, and she was going to be a beaut.

He tried not to stare as the first spatters of rain sizzled into steam when they hit hot asphalt. Rain squalls, or feeder bands, served as warm-up acts for the main event. They would intensify as the hurricane approached. While he was pretty certain Cocoa Beach was battened down, rising winds could turn every loose trash can lid into a spinning saw blade. He needed to make sure that didn't happen.

A freshening breeze pelted his arms and face with sand and drew his attention to the ocean and an approaching squall line. If the first of them was coming ashore, Hurricane Arlene had not made the projected turn. Instead, she had picked up her pace. He would have to do the same.

Brett felt his tires grab as he roared out of the Palm Royale parking lot onto the empty highway. In the next instant, he slammed on the brakes, anti-lock technology bringing the heavy sedan to a rocking, ticking stop. He stared through his windshield in disbelief. In the short time he'd been at the condos, a mountain of flattened cardboard boxes had somehow formed along the roadside. Brett's mouth opened and closed in mute protest.

The mountain was not supposed to be there. It hadn't been there when he'd arrived. And as sure as a rising tide, it wouldn't be there when he left.

STEPHANIE'S HEART leaped when the doorbell chimed. She practically bolted to answer it, until the hurried slap of her sandals against the tile floor sent little echoes bouncing off the walls. Deliberately, she slowed. Pausing for a quick look in the foyer's recently hung mirror, she exchanged her relieved grin for a slightly exasperated expression. She wasn't the one who was five hours late, and she intended to demand a free installation. She wouldn't get it if she went all gushy over the repairman's arrival.

With her features properly schooled, she pulled the door wide, chiding, "It's about time."

The folly of opening a west-facing door into Florida's late afternoon sun hit her square in her unprepared eyes. Feeling as if a dozen flashbulbs had exploded inches from her face, she raised one hand as a shield. No good. A man's tall outline was all she could see against the background of black speckles and white, popping balloons. She quickly averted her eyes, finding relief in the soothing brown shades of variegated pebbles in the Chattahoochee deck. She stared at a pair of shiny, black shoes.

Workmen wore boots, not shoes. Especially not shoes that looked as if they'd been treated to a military spit-shine.

Her eyes headed upward, this time taking in the impossibly long, knife-edge crease of navy uniform slacks. Her vision stuttered at a tightly cinched waist where the hoped-for tool belt looked more like a holstered gun. The large hand resting there sent her pulse racing. Hadn't both hands been at the man's sides when she opened the door? She sped over a broad chest and even broader shoulders to a face overshadowed by the dark brim of a hat and a pair of mirrored sunglasses. Her heart thudded an extra beat.

"Cocoa Beach Police, ma'am. Are you having trouble?"

The deep, rapid-fire rumble yanked her gaze back into the blinding sun so fast the dreaded "ma'am" almost failed to register.

She squinted, trying to see his face but all she got for her trouble was another blast of light.

"Police?" Blinking, she shook her head. "I didn't call the police." Through watery eyes she saw his outline relax a bit, though the man standing on her front porch remained all shadows and glint.

"Sorry, ma'am. When you said 'about time,' I thought you might have car problems or something. Everything is under control, then? You're on your way?"

Stephanie forced her lips into a determined smile and stuffed a growing irritation firmly behind it. Everything was all right, though it wouldn't be if he "ma'am'd" her one more time.

"Yes, Officer, uh—I'm sorry, I didn't catch your name."

"Lincoln, ma'am. Officer Lincoln."

Three ma'ams in a row—it was enough to make any self-respecting twenty-six-year-old cry. She was twenty-six and self-respecting, but she wasn't going to cry, even if the eerie quiet of her new neighborhood had shredded her last nerve and left her as jumpy as two double lattes. Instead, she blinked rapidly to clear the pesky, sun-induced tears and, pulling herself erect, squared her shoulders.

"Pleased to meet you, Officer Lincoln. I'm Stephanie, Stephanie Bryant." She tossed enough ice into her tone so Officer Lincoln would understand they were done with the "ma'am" business. When he tipped his hat, she knew she'd made her point. She spilled a little warmth back into her voice.

"I'm not sure why you'd suspect car trouble, but yes, everything is fine. It will be even finer when the installation guys show up. That's who I was waiting for. I don't suppose you have any pull with the telephone company, do you?"

"No, ma—uh. No, Miss Bryant. But they won't be here today."

That was close, but she'd give him one more chance. Muscular police officers who smelled like piney woods deserved that, even when they seemed determined to argue. Holding her smile firmly in place, she explained, "I know it's almost five, but they promised. I'm sure they've just been delayed."

"Delayed till next week, maybe."

Officer Lincoln reached for his sunglasses. When his posture shifted just enough so the blinding sun disappeared behind his back, Stephanie wondered if the move was a deliberate attempt to make her heart stop. Peering up at a profile so chiseled it might have been carved by Michelangelo, she was pretty sure her breathing had. The man had an almost perfectly proportioned face with a straight nose and barely rounded chin that jutted forward exactly the right amount. Above a strong jawline with the late afternoon stubble of someone who shaved twice a day, tanned skin hugged impressive cheekbones. She followed them to his hairline. Despite its close cropping, the thick, dark hair wanted to curl where the heat and humidity dampened it. She felt an answering, unexpected warmth stir in her chest as, beneath wide slashes of black eyebrows, a pair of black-blue eyes studied her intently.

"Miss Bryant, why are you here?" he asked. "Haven't you been listening to the weather reports?"

Abruptly, the urge to trail her fingers along his cheek's sandpaper stubble disappeared. Stephanie remembered to breathe. She also remembered to cross her arms and take a step back while pondering the seriously flawed nature of the male species. This one might look like a Greek god, but he wasn't listening to her any better than Adonis had listened to Aphrodite. She tried again.

"I just moved in, Officer. I don't have television or cable service because I'm waiting for the installers to show up. And they're late."

"I understand that. But they won't be here. *You* shouldn't be here."

Officer Lincoln glanced over his shoulder at the street. "Are those your packing boxes at the curb?"

"Why? Are you on box patrol?"

She had meant the question as a joke, but Officer Lincoln continued to stare down from his impressive height without even the trace of a smile.

"They can't stay there. You'll have to move them inside."

Stephanie ground her teeth. She had tried to be polite. She had tried to be understanding. She had even tried humor, and look where that had gotten her. It was time to put her foot down.

"Officer Lincoln, I read the brochures. Tomorrow is recycling day. I don't understand the problem."

The man drew a folded handkerchief from his back pocket and took his time polishing the lenses of spotless sunglasses.

"Emergency Management has issued an evacuation order for all the barrier islands," he said. His voice dropped impossibly lower. "That includes Cocoa Beach. You need to get out of here. In fact, you have less than two hours to cross the causeway before it closes, so I'd suggest you get moving."

Stephanie bit her lip to keep from telling Officer Lincoln exactly where he was wrong. This morning the weatherman had said the storm would turn. She had it on good authority that hurricanes never came ashore in Cocoa Beach. Besides, even if Officer Lincoln was correct, the evacuation order was for the barrier islands, and she wasn't on a—

Her heart thudded all the way to her feet as she remembered the maps the real estate agent had provided. Several long fingers of land hugged the Florida coast the way fringe dangled from her pink pashmina. Cocoa Beach sat on one of them.

"Barrier island?" she mouthed.

Images of hurricane-ravaged coastal towns flooded her thoughts. She reached for something to brace herself with, her hands finding and clutching the door frame. Officer Lincoln's lips kept moving, but a sound of rushing water and roaring wind filled her head. She couldn't hear a word he said.

"No," she whispered. This couldn't be happening.

BRETT STARED in disbelief as the compact powder keg in front of him started to smoke. Within seconds there would be an explosion that might take hours to clean up. He didn't have hours. Hurricane Arlene would be on top of them by then. Her one-hundred-and-fifty-mile-an-hour winds could push seven-foot waves clear across Cocoa Beach, and he did not want to get caught in the storm surge.

As protests spiraled upward and a pair of the bluest eyes he'd ever seen widened impossibly, Brett rapidly reviewed his options. Given enough time, he could talk her down. He had the negotiating skills. Problem was, neither of them had the time.

An unexpected shake might jar her to her senses, but that was almost guaranteed to land him in the middle of litigation. Having seen lawyers in action, he'd rather face hurricanes.

That left option number three, another plan sure to land him in trouble. Was she worth it? One quick appraising glance—and more experience than he liked to admit—told Brett all he needed to know.

Hair did not bounce and shimmer the way her glossy, black curls did unless their owner spent considerable time and money in expensive beauty salons. If his last girlfriend was any indication, a complexion so flawless and cheeks such a rosy pink required serious expenditures at the cosmetic counter. Brett took note of the woman's narrow shoulders above lush round breasts. Her tiny waist flared into hips with barely enough meat on them for a man to grasp. He recognized the snug fit of layered Lands' End T-shirts when he saw them, and those strategically frayed capris fit too well to be from Walmart. Expensive clothes to wear on moving day.

He continued his downward assessment, traveling a short distance of thigh to the place where muscular calves tapered into elegant ankles. The woman had good bone structure, he'd give her that, but he knew maintaining such a perfectly proportioned figure meant hours on treadmills and Nautilus machines. The baby-doll-pink toenails in their unscuffed sandals made him grimace.

No doubt about it, she was one of the "me, me" girls. The kind that got his back up, the kind he'd sworn off after his last long-term relationship had self-destructed.

Her lips moved rapidly in a heart-shaped face so perfect it kicked his temperature up a notch. The woman was physically attractive, no sense denying it. But could he ignore her looks long enough to reach a simple conclusion? He could, and he would. If his words were wasted on her, he'd save his breath.

Grasping Miss Stephanie Bryant by the shoulders, he tumbled her forward while slipping his free hand around to his back. In one fluid move, he loosed a pair of handcuffs from his belt and snapped silver around a slim, white wrist.

The petite figure before him immediately stilled and Brett looked down. He had sworn her eyes couldn't get any wider. He was wrong about that.

Chapter Two

A metallic snap and the pinch of cold steel around one wrist stopped Stephanie in midprotest. She flattened her lips in a thin line, every muscle in her body suddenly on alert. Despite the sharp tug she gave her hand, the policeman did not relax his viselike grip.

"H-hey!"

She stared at her hand in its uncomfortable new bracelet while she felt the blood drain from her face. After that, her mind drew a blank. Not that it mattered since her mouth had trouble forming the simplest words. Her eyes darted around, but all she could see was a uniform shirt—the solid expanse blocked her vision in every direction. She shook her head to clear it.

"Officer Lincoln, you've made your point." Even rising corporate executives knew when they'd been bested. "I'll leave."

"I have your word on that?" he asked.

She had always known she was small, but her wrist looked positively fragile in his grip. For half a second, she wondered what it would be like to snuggle up to his chest and let the big man take care of her. The open jaws of the second cuff put a quick end to that fantasy and made her decision to go along with his plan an easy one. Mustering her most sincere look, Stephanie tipped her head back to meet a pair of searching blue eyes.

"I promise," she said. Officer Lincoln had to be mistaken about the storm, and tomorrow's clear skies and tropical breezes would prove her right. Tomorrow, safely ensconced in her corner office she would pick up the phone, her *executive* phone, and have a chat with the police commissioner or the chief of police or whatever the person in charge called himself in small-town Florida. She might even file a complaint against the cop who'd refused to let her spend the night in her own home. But first, she had to get through today.

And today, getting arrested was not part of her game plan. Nor was getting fired because she had a police record. Both would seriously impact her goal of becoming Space Tech's first female CEO. With her job and her latest promotion at risk, a much better alternative would be to climb into her rental car and spend the night at the closest hotel.

"Just let me grab my keys and an overnight bag."

He held on to her hands. "I'll escort you as far as the causeway," he said.

Stephanie's eyebrows rose. "You don't believe me?" Honesty was the touchstone of every business deal. Too bad the broad-shouldered cop didn't recognize the truth when he heard it.

"I am a law-abiding citizen," she pointed out. "I wouldn't lie to you."

"Law-abiding citizens lie," Officer Lincoln argued. His looked pointedly at the handcuffs. "And you have been arrested."

"Not officially," she countered. She gave the cuffs the same kind of shake she would give a troublesome bracelet.

"You haven't read me my rights. If you take this off, I'll grab my things and we can get out of here."

When his cool, appraising eyes did not flicker, she tried again. "Didn't you say we had no time to waste?"

Throwing his words back in his face seemed to do the trick because his eyes definitely wavered.

"All right," he nodded, "but you'll need more than an overnight bag." He unhooked a heavy key ring from his belt and freed her wrist. "Take enough clothes for at least three days. Pack everything you can't afford to lose—insurance papers, heirlooms and jewelry, your grandmother's photograph. You'll need some proof of residency. You can't get back into Cocoa Beach without it. And pack some food. You'll want it."

"Clothes. ID. Important papers. I got it," she said. Pointedly, she rubbed her wrists. As for food, she hadn't been to the grocery store, but she would manage. Dinner in an upscale restaurant would make a nice reward after a day that had so not gone according to plan.

Officer Lincoln stood on the porch until Stephanie opened the coat closet and retrieved her smallest suitcase. "Have it your way," he said. Despite an acquiescent shrug, he lingered.

"Are you going to watch while I pack?" she asked. Her cheeks burned at the thought of the arrogant cop watching as she tossed thongs and skimpy bras into her bag.

Officer Lincoln retrieved his sunglasses from a shirt pocket and slipped them on.

"If you'll open your garage door, *ma'am,* I'll bring those boxes in while you get ready to leave. Make it quick. Ten minutes. Twenty, tops."

Stephanie spun away without bothering to answer. He had ma'am'd her. Again. This time, deliberately. The idea that she could be attracted to someone so full of himself was simply ludicrous, but there was the small matter of her hands to deal with. She wiggled her fingers. Though she tried telling herself the cuffs must have been too tight or Officer Lincoln had held her hands higher than she realized, her skin tingled everywhere he'd touched her.

BRETT KEYED the dashboard mike and spoke to Doris. "I'm at the old Henson place," he said. In the manner of small towns, the house would remain the Henson place for the next ten years, no matter who held the deed.

He opened his mouth to let Dispatch know the new resident required an escort to the causeway just as Stephanie Bryant stepped through the front door. He watched as she lowered a plastic tub into the trunk of her car. When his eyes locked on a fine view of a denim-clad derriere, Brett's mouth clamped shut.

"I'll be tied up for about an hour," he said simply. Anything more and Doris would demand details. At the moment, there were some things he didn't trust himself to report.

By the time he logged off, the fitful breeze had died and the shapely Ms. Bryant had retreated into her air-conditioned lair. Brett hoped she knew how to pack in a hurry. Once the winds picked up, driving across the causeway would be more dangerous than staying in Cocoa Beach. And that could be deadly.

He headed for the stack of flattened boxes at the curb. Even if the best happened and the storm slid up the coast without making landfall, floodwaters were inevitable. Wet cardboard was heavier than dirt and would sprout mold before the next tide receded. With the city practically shut down until the storm passed, it was his civic duty to haul the boxes into the garage. The town's newest resident had nothing to do with it.

Brett swiped his damp forehead. Hurricane Arlene was drawing moisture and heat out of the ocean like a kid sucking on a Slurpee. Until the storm moved close enough to dump her contents on them, the temperature and humidity in Cocoa Beach remained near normal. So it wasn't the weather that had him in a sweat. No, the delectable Stephanie Bryant had done that all by herself.

If attraction was all there was to it, he would simply ask her out. But something about the petite woman stirred his protective side. Maybe it was the sight of her small wrist in his handcuffs. Maybe it was the way her head brushed against his shoulder. Whatever. He was practical enough to look for a logical reason and quickly found one.

No matter what the crime, women always cried.

The first time one of his arrestees turned on the waterworks, he had still been a probationer and partnered with Jake. Brett would have caved under the pressure, but the older cop had seen it all and knowingly ignored the tears of a teenage shoplifter. When Jake proceeded with the girl's arrest, her attitude had done a swift one-eighty and earned him a quick kick to the shins. Brett, a fast learner, had hardened himself against crying females after that incident.

But Stephanie Bryant hadn't cried. He would have spotted so much as a single tear if it had welled in those big blue eyes. Her resolve made her seem all the more vulnerable. When he'd touched her shoulder, it had been all he could do not to draw her into his embrace and whisper reassurance in her ear. From the way she had leaned into him, he was fairly certain she wanted the same. Not that it mattered.

She was wrong for him. Not all wrong, maybe, but wrong enough.

Glossy dark curls and pert red lips might be all right for the next guy, but he had learned a hard lesson from his last relationship with a beautiful woman. The other cops, Jake in particular, had tried to warn him. He hadn't listened, and they had been right about her. At first, Brett hadn't understood why the guys called her a "me, me" girl. He was already in over his head by the time he realized she was all about "me." Me, as in "Honey, don't go fishing. Stay home with me." And, "Sweetie, turn off the basketball game. Pay attention to me."

Stephanie Bryant, with her designer clothes, was the second verse of the same old song. Her beauty came at a price he wasn't willing to pay. No doubt about it.

Whether or not he completed the half-finished master's thesis hidden in his desk drawer, he would remain a beat cop with a beat cop's hours and a beat cop's salary. A desk job was twenty years in his future. And that was okay with him. He liked his work. He spent his free time with other men who viewed the world from the right side of a badge.

So, maybe he hadn't seen Tom, Mary and the girls as much as he should. Maybe he hadn't been fishing in a while. Maybe he had played too much pool and thrown too many darts with the guys at Sticks N Tips. His time at the cop hangout would only last until he got his head on straight about women and relationships.

No, Stephanie Bryant wasn't his type. But he could enjoy the scenery while he toted flattened boxes into her garage.

He slowed his steps for maximum viewing time. She had traded one expensive outfit for another, and though this one was as impractical as the one before it, Brett had to admit she had spent her money well. The plunging neckline of a silky pink camisole revealed enough cleavage to make his mouth water. The lacy hem ended at her waist, a good three inches above the low-riding pants that now hugged her curves. Imagining his hand resting on her smooth skin, he forced his eyes downward before he embarrassed himself. But down was no good, either. Her pink toenails peeked from a pair of sandals that were all straps and impossibly high heels.

"Heaven help me," he mumbled. He rolled his eyes skyward where another line of low clouds gathered. Fifteen of the twenty allotted minutes had passed and the time for sightseeing was over. He needed to hustle Ms. Bryant on her way before the rain squall struck, but in the moment he'd looked away, the brunette had disappeared from sight. Deciding he'd wait a sec before giving her a shout, he posted himself at her car's open trunk.

What people considered too important to lose said a lot about their character. Brett's instincts, honed razor-sharp by four years on the force, told him Ms. Bryant had filled her trunk with mere trivia. Certain that a quick survey would prove him right, he put his assumptions to the test.

She hadn't packed much in the way of clothes, he saw with some surprise. He had expected her to label her closet's entire contents as critical, but a business suit and an overnight bag were all she had added to a trunk filled with boxes and plastic bins. The laptop she had snugged between the boxes and the tire well came as less of a surprise. Even he owned a laptop and he wasn't a "me, me" anything.

Curiosity got the best of him when he saw a cardboard box labeled with the broad strokes of a Magic Marker. He lifted one corner of the lid. The box contained what it said it did and elicited an honest chuckle. Were s'mores something Stephanie Bryant could not afford to lose? Or did she consider sweets one of the four basic food groups? Either way, the items she'd packed told him he might have mis-judged the petite brunette.

The sound of soft footsteps behind him made him drop the lid faster than a hot shell casing. How the woman had snuck up on him he did not know. He hadn't even heard her front door open. Irritation knifed through him at letting her catch him with his guard down and he plas-tered on a hasty smile to cover his guilty look. He spun toward her.

"Want some help?"

"Sure," she answered. The look she tossed his way lit up her face. "If you could put these in the car for me, I'll lock the door."

Brett's smile lost some of its underpinnings when he saw what she carried. In one hand, the soon-to-be-evacuee toted a perfectly acceptable black leather briefcase. From the buffed and groomed fingers of the other dangled a plastic contraption built like a multi-tiered wedding cake. An avocado-green wedding cake filled with a drugstore's entire cosmetic aisle. On its bottom shelf, jars, tubes and cotton swabs crowded behind a guardrail. Brushes and nail files bristled from the top. In between, an army of polish bottles rallied for the call to paint the world baby-doll-pink.

"Huh," Brett groused. So much for misjudging the girl. It was time for him to quit sending mixed signals and strike a professional pose.

He grabbed the briefcase and manicure stand and turned his back on her. The pebbles on the porch made a gritty sound as he pictured Ms. Bryant's weight shifting from one slim ankle to another. She was probably trying to figure out what was going on. He couldn't blame her. He sort of wondered the same thing until he remembered his whole reason for being here. With a hurricane nearing the coast, the barometer was sinking like a lead weight at the end of a fishing line. The change had to be messing with both their heads.

Slipping the briefcase into an empty spot, he paused to consider his next move. The stand did not fit into the tiny space left in her trunk so he was forced to move things around a bit. A nudge to one of the plastic bins revealed a Space Tech logo plastered across its top. The sight sent Brett's stomach into free fall. The remnants of his smile went with it. The files she deemed so important, the things she "couldn't afford to lose," were all work-related. As far as he was concerned, that did it.

Ms. Stephanie Bryant was exactly what he did not need—a self-centered career girl, a girl whose designer labels read Ms. Wrong.

"Ready?" he growled. He didn't bother to turn and face her.

"All set."

He waited until he heard keys jingle and the light tap of her heels. "Did you pack a cot or a sleeping bag? You'll need one."

Like the hurricane building off the coast, her answer drew all the moisture from the air. "I don't know about the hotels you stay in, *Officer* Lincoln, but the Marriott provides linens."

Brett quirked one eyebrow. "Every hotel within a hundred miles of here is filled to capacity," he said. "You have to go to a shelter."

"A shelter?" she snorted. "You've got to be kidding. I'm not homeless."

Too bad she was not his type. He would have enjoyed trading verbal jabs with the feisty little beauty. "A storm shelter," he corrected as he slammed the trunk closed. "The closest one with any openings is in Orlando."

Her incredulous look told him the woman still did not believe Hurricane Arlene was within striking distance. If she didn't believe, she wouldn't run. Something she needed to do. And fast. He latched on to the task.

"Look. See those dark clouds out there?" He pointed to a spot where the clear blue sky ended and slate-gray clouds began. "That's a feeder band. It's the outer edge of a Category 4 hurricane. Arlene's hundred-and-fifty-mile-an-hour winds are going to slam this coast in a matter of hours. You want to be somewhere safe when that happens. There won't be much left standing if we take a direct hit."

He watched her questioning glance wander to the new roof and concrete walls of the house and knew what she was thinking. He'd be thinking the same thing if he hadn't seen, firsthand, the damage previous storms had inflicted. Stephanie Bryant was no match for hurricane-force winds. He needed to give it to her straight so she could understand the danger she faced.

"Your house is not safe. It may not even exist after this hurricane strikes. The hotels are full. The closest shelter is in Orlando. You need to get in your car and drive there. If you waste time by stopping at places along the way, you'll never make it. Trust me on this, you do not want to be on the road when Hurricane Arlene comes ashore. And she's coming!"

As if emphasizing his point, the first splatters of rain fell on the roof of Stephanie's car. It was enough to seal the deal. He watched as she practically bolted for the front seat.

Newcomers, Brett thought as he tromped across the grass to his patrol car. They were all the same. They bought riverfront houses and complained that the mangroves blocked their view. They built new homes in low-lying bogs where mosquitoes swarmed. And, unless someone laid down the law, they put themselves in danger by riding out a hurricane on a barrier island.

As rain pelted his windshield and blew in sheets across the roadway, Brett checked to make sure Stephanie Bryant trailed in the wake of his flashing blue lights. She hung so close to his bumper her pinched and hollow face filled his rearview mirror.

Maybe he had overdone it a touch. It wasn't her fault the season's biggest storm was within striking distance. For the rest of the short drive to the causeway, he chastised himself for his bad behavior and sought a way to make amends.

HANDS GRIPPING the steering wheel so tightly her knuckles paled, Stephanie followed the flashing blue lights down one deserted street after another. Why hadn't she noticed that every house in the beachside community was shuttered or boarded up? That yards were devoid of people because all the smart ones had long since vacated? Even the Jet Skis and small boats that had once sprouted from every drive-way had disappeared. She balled a fist and struck the leather armrest.

She lived on a barrier island.

Okay, so maybe she was better at negotiating a new benefits package than reading a map, but someone—her Realtor came to mind—might have mentioned such an important fact. If she had known it, she would have insisted on a different house. She would have fled for her life as soon as the first alert was issued.

But, no.

She had spent all day unpacking when she should have been driving as fast as she could back to safety. Back to her parents' house where she had lived until her big promotion had come through. Up the stairs and back into her old bedroom with its pink, dotted Swiss wallpaper, frilly curtains and white canopy bed built for one.

Okay, maybe she wouldn't go that far back, but she wouldn't be here, either. Not driving through a vacant city behind the world's most cantankerous cop. A man who insisted she cross two bridges and a narrow spit of land minutes before the world as she knew it was destroyed by a hurricane bearing her middle name.

If that wasn't enough to give a girl wrinkles, nothing would.

Small wonder she could barely speak when Officer Lincoln motioned her to a stop at the base of a bridge. Torrential rain slacked off long enough for him to step from his patrol car without getting soaked. She watched as he grabbed something from his backseat and, pulling his cap low, dashed through the light drizzle and steaming puddles to her car.

"It's a sleeping bag and pillow," he said as he opened the rear door and tossed a bundle onto the seat behind her. "Consider it a peace offering. I know I came on pretty strong at the house. It's my job to get you out of harm's way and keep you safe, but I didn't mean to scare you to death."

So the big burly policeman had a heart. That was a surprise. Stephanie gathered her wits enough to thank him. "I can't take your sleeping bag, though," she said. "You'll need it."

He overrode her protests. "They have cots for us at the station. And don't worry about getting it back to me. I know where you live."

He probably intended the "ah, shucks, ma'am" grin to reassure her, but Stephanie was too busy listening to her heart. It pounded, every beat shouting, "Too late! Too late!" It was too late to run. Too late to get a hotel room. Too late for anything but a nerve-wracking drive into the middle of the state where she hoped to find space in a shelter. She would have floored it all the way to Orlando if she'd known how to get there.

Fortunately for her, Officer Lincoln's thoughts were a tad more organized. He ripped a hand-drawn map from his notepad and handed it through her lowered window. "It's a straight shot from here to the shelter. You have a full tank of gas?"

She nodded mutely.

"A cell phone?"

"Yes, but it doesn't work," she said. The useless device made a dandy paperweight though. With trembling fingers, she used it to anchor the map into the cup holder.

"It will once you reach the mainland. What's your number?" he asked.

She gave it to him while he jotted notes on a pad.

"You'll be all right," he said. His voice dropped like a lifeline through her open window and she clung to it. "Just follow the map and don't take any detours."

His words might have satisfied a Florida girl, but she was from Ohio. She needed more reassurance. She fought an unexpected urge to put Officer Lincoln's oath to serve and protect to the test by burying herself in his muscular arms. His chest certainly looked broad enough to shield her from the coming storm.

"You'll be all right," he repeated. He leaned down until his face was inches from her own.

Wishing she shared his confidence, Stephanie searched for courage and found more than she was looking for in his hooded blue eyes. He leaned a fraction closer. Momentary uncertainty made her check either side of the window where the doorframe supported his weight. Satisfied he wasn't about to slap the cuffs on her a second time, she finally allowed herself to believe she was about to be kissed. How much she wanted it stunned her.

Her breath stalled. Her lips prepared to be met. Her eyelids drifted down and...

The air pulsed with the glow of a distant lightning strike. Thunder clapped its heels and she jerked back. Cold water dashed her face and drowned her brief fantasy as a sudden downpour drenched the man outside her window. Officer Lincoln pulled away from her car as if he'd been slapped, but he gave her a thumbs-up sign and a wide grin. In the instant it took her window to glide home, water had already begun to pour from the brim of his uniform cap. He signaled her onto the roadway.

She watched him shrink in her rearview mirror, knowing he had her back if she needed him. While she couldn't deny how good that felt, she gave her head a stern shake. Kissing the police officer would have been a mistake on so many levels. With her future riding on this move and the new responsibilities that came with it, there was no time in her life for romance. One director had already failed at the job, his name quietly expunged, his job reassigned—to her. This time, Space Tech expected results, not excuses. But her schedule was already in shambles and she hadn't even spent a day behind her new desk. If she couldn't get things back on track—and soon—the only thing she could kiss goodbye was her dream of becoming a corporate executive.

Rain pounded on her windshield. Gray skies filled the eastern horizon. Wind whipped the palms and sent loose fronds skittering across the road. Stephanie cringed as another bolt of lightning struck offshore. Determined to outrun the storm and the need building within her, she pressed harder on the accelerator.

Chapter Three

With the rainstorm raging behind her, Stephanie sped up the westbound ramp onto the Beach Line. From the crest of the next humpbacked bridge she saw nothing but empty road. It told her exactly what she did not want to know— she *was* the last person off the island. A chill prickled her arms and she pressed her foot nearly to the floor until, at last, a set of red taillights appeared in the distance. She paced the car ahead while ominous weather reports spewed from the radio.

As if she needed another reminder of how right Officer Lincoln had been, her cell phone rang the second her tires hit the mainland. Her anxious parents needed reassurance. It was hard to sound breezy and carefree while winds buffeted her car and another squall rattled the roof, but she downplayed the danger and focused on her safety.

"I'm fine," she insisted. When the radio announcer disagreed, she spun the dial until country music filled the car. Carrie Underwood's "Jesus Take the Wheel" wasn't the most reassuring choice, but it was better than the storm warnings.

"I'll be perfectly safe in Orlando. I'm practically there already." She crossed her fingers so her parents wouldn't know she was lying.

Rain squalls stretched the hour-long drive to ninety tense minutes. When she finally steered into the crowded parking lot of the middle school marked on the map Officer Lincoln had given her, her cell phone began to ring insistently. She found a lone vacant slot at the end of the building and blew out a deep breath, promising she would one day thank the man who had evicted her from her house. Before it quit ringing, she grabbed her cell and glanced at the 321 area code and the unfamiliar number.

Was someone from Space Tech calling to warn her of the impending storm? A bit late, she thought, and straightened.

"Stephanie Bryant," she said mustering the most professional voice her frazzled nerves allowed.

"Stephanie, this is Brett. Where are you?"

Her brow puckered. Memorizing all the Space Tech employee names was still on her To Do list, but she was almost certain there was no Brett on the payroll. "I'm sorry. Who is this?"

"Brett. Brett Lincoln."

Oh. Him. She dropped her work voice.

"Brett, huh?" she teased. "So, you have a first name other than 'Officer'?"

"All my life," came the dry response. "Have you reached the shelter yet?"

If a sense of humor lurked beneath that rough cop's exterior, she hadn't found it. She eyed the mortar that ran between the concrete blocks of the shelter's sturdy walls and tried again. "No, I decided to ride it out at the house."

His response was immediate. "Not a chance. Your place is locked up tight and your car isn't there."

The jury was still out on the humor thing, but he had checked. Concern was also a good quality.

"Don't worry. You made a believer out of me. I've just

arrived at the shelter and I'm headed inside as soon as we finish. Anything new on the weather reports?" The constant hurricane warnings had been so unnerving she had opted to stick with the country western station broadcasting from someplace called Ocala.

Brett's voice deepened. "They say the eye will come ashore before daylight."

Stephanie gulped. An intercom crackled in the background and Brett asked her to hold. The interruption gave her a chance to pray that her Cocoa Beach home would still be there when she got back.

"I have to go," Brett said.

There was something else she needed to say. "Um, if I haven't told you already, thanks. Thanks, for everything."

"Yeah, well. Just part of the job."

She thought it might be more than that and wondered if he did, too. "Stay safe," she said.

"As safe as I can be," he replied and disconnected.

Her thoughts raced back to the bridge. If the rain squall hadn't hit at that moment, would she have made a complete idiot of herself? Thoughts of dark hair and chiseled features kicked her heart rate into overdrive.

This was so not good.

She'd bet money that a long-haul kind of guy lurked beneath all that bluster. Trouble was, she wasn't a long-haul kind of gal. Relationships were a distraction and simply did not figure into her foreseeable future. Brett Lincoln might be someone to build a life with, but she she'd be moving on soon.

Space Tech had given her a huge promotion, moved her across the country, provided a house to live in and a thousand other perks. In exchange, the company expected results. Positive ones. Results that hurricanes and hunky cops threatened to undermine.

The timing couldn't be worse. She shook her head.

Cocoa Beach's finest might as well be wrapped in crime scene tape labeled Police Line, Do Not Cross. Her commitment to Space Tech was the only relationship she could afford. Her career—and her future—depended on it.

She stifled a groan as a fresh crop of splatters hit the windshield. Dreaming of the unattainable was not going to keep her safe. She got out of the car and dashed through the rain to a wide covered walkway where smokers had congregated. Spindly legs pumping and torn canvas sneakers splashing through puddles, a woman whose polyester shirt ended at midthigh over a pair of biking shorts headed toward Stephanie before she had a chance to shake the drops from her umbrella. The woman aimed a nicotine-stained thumb toward a set of oversize double doors and blew smoke and information with the same breath.

"The registration desk is just inside, but you might want to unload your car first. Looks like we're gonna get wet and there's no tellin' when it'll let up again. You want some help?"

Stephanie glanced from the woman to the rapidly darkening sky and back to the ID badge that lay nearly horizontal across her ample chest.

"Sure, Judy," she said. "That'd be nice."

Judy Evers kept the monologue flowing between puffs until they reached the car. "You can fill out a form and leave it on the table. Rules are on the table, too. Just pick a spot anywhere and spread out your stuff. You're too late for dinner, but there's sandwiches in the kitchen if you're starving." She bent to dip the nub of her smoke in a nearby puddle and rubbed the butt between her fingers until it flaked as Stephanie opened the trunk.

Judy took a quick look. "You're not going to take all this stuff inside?"

It was not a question Stephanie knew how to answer. "Brett, um… The police said not to leave anything important at the house. Too much, huh?"

"There's not a lot of room," Judy cautioned. "And you have to watch your stuff, though we don't have too many problems. Those file boxes will probably be just as safe in your car as they would be inside. That a laptop?" She paused long enough for Stephanie to give a brief nod. "Leave it here unless you're prepared to watch it every second."

So much for getting some work done while she waited out the storm. "Fine," she said. "Whatever you think." It had been a long, tiring day. If she couldn't work, she'd settle for someplace safe and quiet until the danger passed.

"You got a pillow? A blanket?" Judy asked.

"Oh, yeah," she said, remembering. While she retrieved the bedroll from her backseat, Judy grabbed a few things from the trunk and splashed through puddles toward the school.

Stephanie eyed the manicure stand swinging from the woman's grasp. How on earth had that gotten into the car? Thinking back, she realized she had succumbed to hurricane mania at the end there, throwing anything within reach into the trunk. But a manicure stand? What else had she packed? And what had she left behind? After grabbing her overnight bag, she hit the lock button on the remote and caught up to her talkative new friend.

Judy had run out of breath and steam by the time her feet struck the protected sidewalk again. She set her bundles on the cement, lit another cigarette, brushed a handful of snarled hair behind one ear and fired questions. "Where're you from, sugar? Hit any bad weather? You all by yourself?"

Stephanie decided not to rehash the trip's harrowing details, but there was no denying that she was alone.

"Come on." Judy's words floated on white smoke. "I'll show you the way." Hoisting the stand and a cardboard box with a loud sigh, she dropped her third cigarette of the quarter hour into another smoker's soda can. "Next year, we'll demand ashtrays," she said to a rail-thin man.

"Promises, promises," came a graveled response. "That's what you said last year."

"Last year?" Stephanie felt her stomach drop. "People have to evacuate every year?"

Judy's barking laugh was half cough. "More like two or three times a month. But only in the summer, sug."

"And sometimes in the fall." The thin man's caveat earned a nod or two from those lingering on the walkway.

Hurricanes did not hit Cocoa Beach. According to her Realtor, a direct strike was as unlikely as a meteor hitting Earth. But people evacuated…*often?*

Stephanie rolled her neck to ease the tension. A headache brewed. A couple of aspirin and a few hours of peace and quiet were a sure cure, but noise rolled out of the school like a wave when Judy tugged on one of the doors. Stephanie cringed.

So much for peace and quiet.

Several hundred noisy evacuees filled the cafeteria. A raised stage dominated one side, where small groups played board games or cards at long tables. On the other, families had staked out sleeping areas the way miners staked their claims, marking personal space with piles of belongings packed in everything from American Tourister luggage to black garbage bags. Televisions blared from AV stands in the four corners, and children were everywhere. Some played or sat or quietly napped despite the din. Others contributed to it.

Stephanie glanced over her shoulder, considering.

Behind her, rain poured from the sky. A strengthening wind drove it halfway across the covered walkway. Thunder clapped on the heels of a bright flash, and she saw several of the smokers hurriedly drown cigarettes and move to the doors. Outside was not the place to be. Squaring her shoulders, she trailed the shelter worker down a haphazard aisle until they reached a bare patch of floor.

"This is a good spot," Judy declared. Before Stephanie had a chance to agree or disagree, her temporary home had been established. "Come on up front soon as you can. There's some papers for you to fill out. Bathrooms are over there." She pointed. "And the kitchen is behind the stage. Hungry?"

Stephanie took stock. An aeon had passed since the morning's bagel. In the car, hunger had gnawed at her. But the stale cafeteria air smelled of too many people, cleaning supplies and a million school lunches. "I could use some coffee," she said.

"Yeah, well, there's plenty of it. I'll meet you up front. You go ahead and get settled."

She should be getting settled in her new home. Maybe meeting a neighbor or two.

Stephanie blinked back frustrated tears. She wanted to crawl between the soft sheets of her own bed. Not spread a borrowed sleeping bag across a linoleum floor. Not unwrap the sweatshirt and small pillow Brett Lincoln had tucked inside. She pressed gray flannel to her face, hoping a whiff of his aftershave would clear her head and give her strength. But the shirt smelled of soap instead of the spicy, woodsy scent she hoped for. She wrinkled her nose and put it aside.

A ripple of excitement brought her head up. People were moving to the corners of the crowded room, gathering beneath the television sets. When she overheard someone say there was an update from Miami, she scrambled to join the rest.

The room quieted as serious-faced television announcers spoke about projected paths and wind speeds. One of them displayed a map of Florida with a red funnel aimed directly at Cocoa Beach. Though the announcers hedged their predictions with "as near as we can tell" and "our best estimate," they concluded that Hurricane Arlene could still make a last-minute turn. On the screen, the funnel tilted and curved north.

Stephanie wanted to ask if that meant they could go home. Her question was answered when the screen switched to a reporter who stood against a backdrop of black sky. He ducked when palm fronds sailed past.

"Stay indoors," he cautioned.

Next came a woman who aimed her camera into the darkness where she said trees had fallen. She repeated the warning to stay inside.

Stephanie watched a replay of the reports. Apparently the Hurricane Center issued updates four times daily. The rest was just fill—excited weathermen standing in gusty rain telling everyone else it was too dangerous to venture outdoors. When the official report began its third replay, she eased her way out of a clump of people who stared at the screen as if in a hypnotic trance.

She rubbed her throbbing temples. Everyone seemed to know more than she did. It was irritating and it was giving her a headache and headaches always put her in a foul mood. She swept the room looking for a distraction that would lift her spirits, but she was doomed. There was nothing even faintly amusing about her situation…unless the clothes thing counted.

She had failed the evacuation dress code. Big time. She

would have to offer a class at Space Tech before the next hurricane struck. Calling it Evacuations for New Hires she would teach, "Avoid all sense of style. Go for the comfort of polyester over linen, stained T-shirts rather than lacy camisoles." Denim was permitted, but never worn cropped and pocketed and definitely not formfitting.

She glanced at Brett's sweatshirt where it lay atop her overnight bag. A mile long and two miles wide, the jersey made perfect evacuation wear. She slipped the gray flannel on over her own shirt. The sweats' arms and hem dangled nearly to her knees, but she rolled the cuffs to her wrists. Cropped pants and strappy shoes still earned her a C-minus in EW, aka Evacuation Wear, but the sweatshirt was warm and cozy. She even felt her headache ease a bit.

Five minutes and a few directions later she sat at the registration table holding a cup of hot coffee. She thumped the dull end of a pen against the table's yellow Formica top and stared at a blank line where she was supposed to provide contact information. The realization that her next of kin were thousands of miles away triggered a wave of vulnerability she hated.

How had she, an Ohio girl—a city girl—ended up in a hurricane shelter? Her Realtor, that's how. Stephanie had believed the woman, who'd said she needn't fear a direct strike. If that wasn't a lie, the forecasters would claim it was "too close to call."

She shook her head before bending to dutifully provide the requested information. The copy of shelter rules looked simple enough. No alcohol, no firearms, no pets, no sex. She looked down at herself, swathed in acres of gray flannel.

Sex was so not an issue.

But someone had an issue and from the sound of things, it was serious. Stephanie honed in on an argument taking place at the entrance where Judy stood with one hand braced against the doorjamb and an unlit cigarette dangling from the other. Her strident voice rose above the general din. "I said that's not allowed. You can't bring it in here."

Stephanie half expected to see someone at the door toting a gun or a case of liquor. But instead what she saw was a bedraggled family. The parents each held a whimpering toddler. Rain dripped from their sodden clothes.

Did Judy mean to keep them out? That wasn't right.

Realizing she had missed something, she searched for the object of contention. At the man's feet sat a dog with sad brown eyes and glistening wet hair.

"No dogs allowed," Judy insisted. "And he can't stay in the car by himself. You'll have to leave."

At this, one of the toddlers let out a loud wail. "No, Daddy, no! Don't let the hurr'cane blow Sem'nole away!" Her mirror image chimed in with another cry, "The hurr'cane will get us if we go outside!"

"He's well-behaved, ma'am," the father argued tiredly. "Please. We need to stay here."

Judy's arms crossed, her intentions plainly visible.

Stephanie was on her feet almost before she realized it. At last—she had found something she could handle.

"Hey!" she shouted on her way to the door. "What took you so long? I was so worried about you." She reached the disheveled family and leaned in to hug the mother. "Just play along," she whispered.

"The kennel gave away our reservation." The explanation sounded like a confession between best friends. "We tried several others—we've been driving around for hours—but no luck. We had to bring Seminole with us."

A skeptical Judy interrupted. "Stephanie, you know these people?"

"They're my neighbors," she said though she had no idea where these "neighbors" actually lived. "Oh, you must be exhausted!" She gave the father a quick hug and smiled brightly at the distraught towheads. "There's plenty of room next to my stuff. You guys can settle in there."

"No," Judy argued. "They can't."

Stephanie ignored her and looked down. "Seminole, I didn't forget you. You're such a good boy. Lie down, now."

The dog was prone in an instant. With the retriever supplying all the confirmation she could hope for, Stephanie decided the situation required a well-placed lie. Maybe two. Dredging up the tone usually reserved for recalcitrant employees, she turned to the shelter manager.

"Judy, Seminole is a companion dog. He's been specially trained as a mother's helper. With these two precious little ones, you can see why anyone would need an extra pair of hands. Or, in this case, feet."

"We sure do," the father piped in. "He's especially gentle around children. He won't be a problem, I swear."

Stephanie hoped their earnestness would put the manager on the fence.

Judy's doubtful look traveled over the group. "I can see that he's well-behaved, but our rules don't allow pets. If you're saying he's a guide dog or something, can you prove it? Don't they all wear vests? Where's his?"

"You didn't think you'd need it at the kennel, did you?" Stephanie prompted.

"Oh, Stephanie, it's my fault." The mother's trembling voice let everyone know honest tears weren't that far away. "I was in such a rush to get out of the house that I walked out and left it on the kitchen table."

Judy's voice dropped so low no one outside their immediate circle could hear. "I don't believe you for a minute, but if you swear this dog will behave himself—" She paused, waiting. One by one, three adults and two children gave solemn nods while the Lab's eyes flicked from one face to another as though he knew his fate was being determined.

"Companion dogs are exempt from the No Pets rule," Judy announced at last. "He'll be confined to your space. If he makes a mess—" she squinted one eye and pursed her lips "—I expect you to clean it up immediately."

"We will, but he won't," the father agreed.

"All right, then." Judy turned to Stephanie. "You get them settled. Make sure they fill out the registration forms."

"Sure thing," Stephanie said. Beckoning, she led the way to her pallet.

"I'm Tom, by the way," the father whispered as they threaded down winding aisles. "This is my wife, Mary. The girls are Barbara and Brenda."

"Good to know," Stephanie said with a chuckle. "And you must be Seminole," she said to the dog who tagged along at Tom's heels. "Where are you guys from?"

"Cocoa Beach," answered Mary.

Stephanie's chuckle became a laugh. "We really are neighbors. I just finished moving in there today. Do you think I should thank the mayor for rolling out the red carpet?" With a sweep of her hand, she indicated the bare patch of floor next to her few boxes. "Definitely not the Ritz. The Marriott, either. But it's dry."

While the girls clung tightly to their parents' necks, Tom and Mary lingered on the threshold of their temporary home. Profuse thanks were offered and declined, but no one seemed certain what they should do next—no one except Seminole. He followed his nose straight to Stephanie's sleeping bag where he helped himself to a good long sniff before plopping down on the floor beside it with an audible sigh. His ease made the girls laugh and soon they were toddling around examining their patch of linoleum.

Stephanie left her newfound friends to embark on a brief scavenger hunt. She returned bearing towels, blankets, hot coffee and juice boxes. While Mary and Seminole watched the girls, she and Tom donned plastic garbage bags turned ponchos—another useful evacuation fashion tip—and raced to unload necessities from the van before the storm worsened. By the time the girls were in their jammies and pallets had been spread across the floor, rain pummeled the roof relentlessly, and the wind blew in powerful gusts.

Hurricane Arlene was nearing the coast.

Local weathermen reported a rapid decrease in barometric pressure, and someone turned up the volume on the television sets. A new edginess spread throughout the cafeteria as evacuees realized the hoped-for turn had not occurred. Voices raised. Arguments broke out. Children grew fussier. Rain drummed the roof.

Stephanie's headache renewed its steady pounding until all she wanted was to curl up in a ball somewhere. Not an option. Copious amounts of chocolate were her fall back remedy. Grumbling about mothers who always knew best, she unearthed the box Judy had toted from the car. She had no idea why it, intended for the local food bank, was in her trunk, but she was mighty glad to see it. Inside sat her mom's idea of a housewarming gift—enough graham crackers, chocolate bars, marshmallows and canned fuel to make s'mores for an army. Tom, Mary and the girls joined her, and they set everything up on one of the cafeteria tables.

The first marshmallow was barely warm before a gawky teen stood at Stephanie's elbow. Told he needed to contribute something—anything—to the table, he quickly returned with a liter of soda. As soon as he walked away with a plate of s'mores and soft drink in a small cup, the game was on. By the time Stephanie opened the second box of crackers, people were helping themselves to a smorgasbord of treats that littered the long row of tables.

With her headache in abeyance, Stephanie turned the s'more making over to Tom and another father. It seemed a pity to waste the good mood running through the room so she commandeered likely looking parents and, with Mary's help, organized several "camp fires." Soon teenagers sat at one and swapped ghost stories. A pre-school teacher volunteered to lead another group in children's songs. Other kids played charades. And watchful adults circulated, quietly updating each other on the storm's status.

Stephanie was bouncing Barbara—or was it Brenda?—on her lap and singing what had to be the twenty-fifth round of "The Wheels On The Bus," when word spread that Hurricane Arlene had finally turned her devastating winds away from Florida. Relief swept the room. Fatigue followed closely on its heels, and the party quickly wound down. As she and Mary carted the girls to their makeshift beds, she asked the question on everyone's mind.

"How soon will they let us go home?"

Mary shifted a sleeping toddler and spoke quietly. "It's hard to say. It depends on the extent of the damage, especially to the causeways."

"But if the hurricane turned…" Stephanie began.

Mary tucked one twin between blankets and reached for her sister. "Even in a near miss, there's damage. Just not

as much. Power lines will be down for sure. It may take
days to get electricity restored. And some of the roads
were probably buried or washed away."

Stephanie stared. "How do you stand it? Evacuating—
what? Two, three times a year? Not knowing what you'll
find when you get back."

"I've lived here all my life. You get used to it. Besides,
the damage usually isn't that bad, and when it is, we hear
something before we get home." At Stephanie's questioning look, Mary added, "Tom's best friend is a cop. He's on
duty tonight and as soon as the sun comes up, he'll tell us
how bad things are." She yawned. "Excuse me," she apologized.

The exhausted look on Mary's face kept Stephanie from
mentioning that she also knew a Cocoa Beach police
officer. She said a quick good-night and followed the
young mother's example by crawling into her own sleeping
bag.

Brett's sleeping bag, she corrected. Juniper and spice
wafted in the air. Stephanie curled into the scent and was
immediately asleep.

Morning meant leftovers from the sweet feast for those
who wanted them, cold cereal for the rest and long delays.
Up and down the east coast, businesses remained closed,
schools on holiday. In the shelter, discussion centered
around the extent of damage. Stephanie ignored the talk
until television reporters began spouting estimates in the
millions. She nearly hit her own panic button before Mary
intervened.

"How do they know?" the young mother pointed out.
"The causeways are closed. No one has access to the
beach. Let's wait for official word before we go too crazy."

Stephanie grabbed a nail file and sank, cross-legged,

onto Brett's sleeping bag where she sawed on the jagged remains of a sculpted nail. She was nearly finished when a serious-faced Tom crossed to his wife's side and wrapped her in a warm embrace. When he whispered something in her ear, Mary buried herself in his arms. They clung together for a long moment while the twins played at their feet.

Watching them, Stephanie felt a hole open in her heart. *I want that,* she thought before catching herself. There was the little matter of finding a likely candidate. She knew exactly one man in Cocoa Beach—Brett Lincoln. Though thinking of him made her pulse jump and his face gave new meaning to *America's Most Wanted,* the policeman had slapped her in handcuffs and threatened her with arrest. He was not her Mister Right.

I want that, but not now, she corrected. Not until after I get my feet on the ground at Space Tech. Not till…sometime.

She was so lost in thought she didn't see Tom until he kneeled beside her.

"Stac—uh, Stephanie. The roads are officially closed," he said quietly. "But I'm pretty sure I can get us back into Cocoa Beach. Mary and I are going to pack up and get out of here in a bit."

Stephanie's breath caught in her throat. "You've, um, heard from your friend, then? How are…things?"

"Not nearly as bad as the reporters would have you believe." Tom grinned. "I run a small marina and we have some damage—nothing we can't fix. The power's still out and the roads won't open for a day or so, but my pal can get us through. How about you? Want to blow this taco stand?"

And get back to work before everyone else? Was he kidding? Even one extra day would give her the time she needed to get her schedule back on track. It would take hard work, but she'd prove that Space Tech had chosen the right person for the job. Stephanie squelched an impulse to jump to her feet and kept her voice low.

"I'm right behind you, but you probably want to keep this quiet?" Tom's nod told her she had accurately judged the situation. "I just have a couple of boxes and a sleeping bag. Why not leave Seminole and me to watch the girls while you and Mary load the van."

There was nothing like a good plan for getting things done. While Mary and Tom reversed the unloading process, Stephanie, much to the delight of the twins, grabbed two bottles of soft pink polish and painted twenty fingernails and twenty toenails.

Chapter Four

Stephanie kept enough pressure on the gas pedal to breeze through the unmanned tollbooth seconds behind Tom and Mary's van. She crested an overpass, the closest thing Central Florida had to a hill. Looking out across the landscape, she could see pine trees that had been snapped like toothpicks. Cattle pastures on either side of the highway stood knee-deep in water. The inky surface sprouted islands of fan-shaped plants and scraggly bushes. In the distance, the Beach Line glistened.

She pressed on, trusting Tom to stop if the road was flooded.

Heat mirages shimmered, but the Beach Line stayed dry all the way to I-95 where their cars were turned aside. They joined convoys of utility vehicles that crowded the southbound lanes of the interstate. Tom led the way past flatbed trucks heavily loaded with Caterpillars and bulldozers from the Carolinas. They steered around a line of power trucks from Alabama.

Canvas flapping, National Guard troop carriers thundered along like the cavalry coming to the rescue. Uniformed men gave casual waves from the backs of green jeeps and buses. Returning their greetings, Stephanie swallowed tears.

She followed Tom onto surface streets, her stomach tightening as they detoured around downed trees that hadn't already been cleared by volunteers wielding chain saws. Along the river, the wind had ripped shutters from condos that had once looked impervious but now sported gaping black holes. A woman stopped sweeping debris from her balcony long enough to wave as their little caravan eased through a low spot where water covered their hubcaps. It was slow going until they reached a line of orange-and-white barricades at the entrance to the causeway. There, state troopers ordered them to halt.

Tom stepped from his car. The men spoke and calls were made, but the wait stretched out so long Stephanie felt sure Tom's influence wouldn't get them past the barricades and onto the road beyond. Wondering if Brett would have better luck, she reached for her cell phone just as a scowling deputy motioned her car forward. Once he verified her street address over the radio, he read from a checklist.

"I have to let you through, but there are rules," grumbled the officer who was *so* disappointingly not Brett.

"Sand drifts cover some roads, so drive with care. There's no electricity, which means no traffic lights. Treat every intersection like a four-way stop. Drinking water and roof tarps are available at the community center. Before you hire anyone, ask to see their business license."

Stephanie's thoughts stuttered to a halt midway through the speech. "Roof tarps?"

"More rain comin'." He jerked a thumb toward a sun-drenched sky. "If your roof has a hole in it, you'll want to cover it with a tarp to minimize water damage."

"Ooo-kaay." She sure hoped that wasn't necessary. "Any idea when we'll get the power back?"

"Several days, at least." The man's frown deepened. "That's one reason we'd rather you stay on the mainland."

His point made, he waved her onto the narrow causeway that led to Cocoa Beach. By then, worry about what she would find there burned fiercely at the base of her throat. With the river a sea of whitecaps on either side of the road, her anxiety ratcheted higher with every mile.

Each wave sheared off a new piece of a partially submerged sailboat. Where the causeway met A1A, the market where she'd bought coffee the day before looked okay, but only rubble marked the spot where an ice cream parlor had once stood. When Tom and Mary waved and turned north, Stephanie's hand and stomach fluttered in return. How much she would see of her new friends remained in doubt but she resisted the urge to follow them. She headed south, her fingers crossed.

A short drive down the coast and she was staring in pleasant disbelief at a sturdy little house that sat right where she had left it. All red roof tiles present and accounted for, peach stucco unscathed. Even the storm shutters had held. Stephanie breathed a thankful prayer.

Inside, she reached for the light switch, but no one could be that lucky. She rocked back on her heels and considered the shutters which had so admirably kept hurricane-force winds at bay. Now, they barred both light and ocean breezes. The temperature was in the nineties…and climbing. So was the humidity level. Even the walls sweated. She could wait for help to come along, but ever since Brett Lincoln had appeared on her doorstep, she'd been relying on other people. That was not the way she usually operated. Certainly not the way she had climbed onto Space Tech's corporate ladder. It was time she started fighting her own battles again.

"You can do this," she said to hear the words. Grabbing several tools, she headed outside.

An hour later, she leaned from her ladder's top step, slid the tip of a screwdriver into a slot and gave it another turn. "Ow!" She winced as a piece of rounded pink acrylic popped off her finger. It flew into the grass at her feet. The shutter would not, could not, win. If she had to wear bandages on all ten fingers when she reported to work, so be it. She tried again.

This time the screwdriver spun in her sweat-slicked hand and joined her fingernail in the grass. Gritting her teeth, she reached into her back pocket. The ground below already looked like a dartboard and if she dropped her last screwdriver, she would have to clamber back down to retrieve the entire set.

Intent on her task, she barely acknowledged the rust-colored truck that pulled to the curb. The two men who emerged must, after all, be her neighbors in the truest sense of the word. Otherwise, they couldn't have gotten past the roadblock. They stepped into place on either side of her window.

"Here now," one of them said. "Need to take the weight off it or the screw won't budge. We'll lift the panel while you turn."

With their help, the shutter she had struggled with slid to the ground.

"Hey, thanks." Climbing down, she brushed damp hair from her face, swiped her hand on her pants and greeted the new arrivals. "I'm Stephanie Bryant. You live around here?"

"Couple of streets over. I'm Dick. This here's my friend Sam." Dick eyed the rest of the house. "Whew! You trying to do all this yourself?"

Though she sensed no threat in the disbelieving smiles

the men traded, Stephanie hedged. "My friend ran to get drinking water and ice. He'll be back soon."

Dick gestured to the boarded-up windows. "The two of us can make quick work of these shutters if you want. We got all the right tools out in my truck 'cause we just finished taking down our own. Be nice to get some air blowin' through the house, wouldn't it?"

Stephanie was all for ocean breezes, but she recognized a business deal in the works. "How much?"

Dick scuffed his toe through the grass and her collection of screwdriver darts. "Well, we wouldn't charge much, seeing as we're neighbors and all." He stopped to think about it. "Fifty sounds about right. That okay with you?"

Fifty dollars to remove a houseful of shutters sounded more than fair. "Okay," she agreed.

At Dick's nod, Sam produced a battery-operated tool and went to work removing the next panel.

"That's fifty…each," Dick said.

Still fair, thought Stephanie. A day at a nice spa cost at least that much. Behind her, the second shutter slid down. Sam moved on.

"Plus expenses."

"Expenses?" She spun away from the house to face the man who was fast losing his neighborly appeal. "What expenses?"

"All right. Five hundred an' we'll eat the extra costs if there are any."

She could move into a first-class hotel for that price. "Stop!" she called.

Dick cupped a hand to one ear as though he had suddenly gone deaf. She motioned to Sam who paid no attention and kept right on working. Another shutter slid from a window.

Stephanie stomped the ground, frustration mounting when her foot sank soundlessly into the spongy grass. She shouted loud enough to make herself heard above the noisy drill.

"I said stop! I am not paying you a dime. Get off my property, and do it now." Even as she issued the order, she wondered what she would do if the two men refused.

What would *they* do? She didn't think she wanted to know the answer and, thanks to the green-and-white cruiser that pulled to the curb behind good ol' boy Dick's truck, she wouldn't have to find out. Her very own cavalry had arrived wearing the uniform of the Cocoa Beach police. Despite the hat pulled low and eyes hidden behind mirrored sunglasses, she recognized Brett Lincoln's tall frame and muscular chest.

Her breath caught. Adonis had never looked so good.

BRETT KEYED his mike.

"Dispatch, this is Lincoln requesting a 10-28 on a Ford pickup bearing Tennessee license plate XAP 195."

After a pause, Doris responded. "Tennessee license plate XAP 195 registered to a 2001 Ford Ranger. Red. Owned by R. J. Johnson. No wants, no warrants."

Which only meant R. J. Johnson had not been arrested in the Sunshine State. Brett sniffed the air. Beneath the salty tang of the ocean, he smelled trouble.

"Doris, I'll be at the Henson place for a bit."

"Roger that."

No banter. No playful flirting. He missed it but Doris, like the rest of the police force, was feeling the strain of thirty-six stormy hours.

He had managed one brief, uncomfortable nap on a folding cot. With no pillow or blanket, the only way he had slept at all was by imagining Stephanie Bryant ensconced in the storm shelter and wrapped in the cocoon of his sleeping bag. Now she was back. How she had gotten through the roadblock and onto the beach he did not know, but he had heard Dispatch verify her street address…before the roads were safe or the power lines up on their poles. He had been fighting the urge to swing past ever since.

From the look of things, he had given in just in time.

Brett's blood chilled when the brunette stomped her foot and argued with two men he did not recognize. Emerging from the cruiser, he caught her eye and gave his head a slight shake.

She was a smart one, that Stephanie Bryant. She did not betray his presence while a drill whined loud enough to cover his nearly silent approach. He didn't speak until his hand rested on his nightstick and he stood directly behind the apparent leader. Only then did he let his voice carry.

"Good afternoon."

The whine died instantly as Brett's thoughts flashed to tomorrow's prospective headlines—Cocoa Beach Officer Killed By Electric Screwdriver. "Not today," he breathed. He motioned said screwdriver to the ground.

"Miss Bryant. Gentlemen. How is everyone?" He asked the question without letting his eyes drift from the leader who spun to face him as soon as the man realized they had company. Brett had jotted down height and weight estimates before he left the car. Now he noted the three-day beards, rumpled clothes and sturdy athletic shoes. Thug Number One wore his sandy blond hair in a fashionable cut that hung over his blue eyes. Number Two had a shaved head. Brown eyes. No visible tattoos. The men looked like any two of a thousand returning homeowners. "Shutters giving you trouble?"

"A bit." Stephanie gestured. "I was trying to remove the storm shutters when these two men, Dick and Sam, showed up. They offered to help, but wanted to charge for the job. We couldn't agree on a price and I asked them to leave. They would not."

In Brett's mind the report was succinct and straightforward, but Thug Number Two—aka Sam—showed his displeasure by shooting a stream of tobacco juice across the lawn.

"Now that's not quite right, ma'am." Number One, the one who called himself Dick, sent his partner a warning glance. "We're doing this as a favor. Neighbor to neighbor." He swung a wounded look toward Brett. "We just asked her to cover our expenses an' we agreed on a price. But when she seen how easy our expertise and specialized tools made the job, she tried to back out." His voice rose. "Ain't that right, Sam?"

Sam nodded. "'Bout sums it up." He spit again.

It was an old scam, one where Brett knew the rules. The cons would lowball the price for a simple job, then increase it for one reason or another until the mark "flinched" or indicated they had reached their limit.

"I have storm shutters at my place," he said thoughtfully. "I'll be too busy the next few days to take them down." He gave Dick a just-between-us-guys look. "How much would you charge for the job?"

"Fifty dollars," said Dick.

"Five—five hundred," Stephanie sputtered.

Brett pretended to hear only one answer. He reached for his back pocket. "Seems fair. So, if I pull a fifty-dollar bill out of my wallet right now and hand it to you, you and your friend here would finish taking down all these shutters?"

"We-ell." Dick drew himself as tall as he could. "We

were just trying to be neighborly, but she has impugned our reputation. Plus, we have to cover expenses. Gas ain't cheap. And it takes special equipment to do the job right."

"Impugned." Brett nodded in apparent sympathy. "Batteries. Drill bits. Maybe a generator?" he suggested.

"Yeah," Dick agreed.

Brett had heard enough. He tightened his grip on the top of his nightstick and squared his shoulders. "So what is it? A favor for a neighbor? Or a job for hire?" One required proof of residency, the other a business license. Either would spell trouble for Dick and Sam, and everyone within sight knew it.

Dick's shoulders slumped. "Tell you what," he offered. "We'll leave. We won't charge the missus for the work we've already done. And we'll just go."

Brett nodded. "Also a reasonable offer. One we should take you up on. I'll notify Dispatch to expect your truck at the roadblock in say—" he pretended to look at his watch "—fifteen minutes. You make it and keep on going, we'll have no further dealings together. You don't make it, or decide to come back, and I'll have to ask some tough questions about your license and permits. Maybe look into your other activities in the state. Do we have an understanding?"

Dick blew out a deep breath. "Yeah. Pack it up, Sam. We're outta here."

Brett stopped the bald man on his way to the pickup. "I'll take those screws, if you don't mind."

"Man can't make a decent living," Sam muttered. He spat—carefully—downwind before dumping the bolts and screws into Brett's hand.

Brett dogged their heels until the two men were on their way and the rest of the force was notified. As he watched them turn the corner, he reached beneath his cap to mop his forehead. His hand came away wetter than expected. He swigged water from a bottle on the front seat of his patrol car. Usually he was immune to the heat, and the altercation with the con men was a part of his daily routine. So what had him so uptight he was sweating?

The answer stood waiting next to the house. At the station last night, and on patrol this morning, he had half convinced himself that Stephanie Bryant was nobody he cared about. A "me, me" girl with a so-so figure and a snippy attitude. Definitely not his style. But one look at her, and he wanted to snug her into his arms and keep her safe. He took another pull from the water bottle, trying to rinse away the bitter taste of adrenaline.

"Are you all right?" he called.

She looked better than all right. She wore workout clothes—by some famous designer, no doubt. Thin jersey stretched tightly across her ample chest. The pants clung in all the right places, right down to the spot where they ended on her shapely calves. The sun had slicked her skin and dampened her hair, turning it into a mass of dark ringlets he wanted to run his fingers through. He crossed the lawn again so they wouldn't have to shout at each other.

"I'm fine," she answered with a nod in the direction the truck had gone. "They seemed harmless enough. I was handling it."

She had grit, he'd give her that. Not every woman would tackle the heavy shutters on her own, or recognize a con when she saw one. But unless people stomped and waved to resolve arguments where she came from, she was wrong about the "handling it" part. What would have happened if he hadn't come along when he had? The back of his neck grew hot again. His voice gruffer than intended, he asked, "Didn't they warn you at the checkpoint about hiring con artists?"

"I didn't hire them," she protested. "They were doing me a favor." She pushed a tangle of curls from her face and her expression fell. "Or, at least, that's how it started. So why didn't you arrest them?"

"Got here a little too early. No money had changed hands. Ergo, no crime had been committed." He didn't like the glum look she wore any better than he liked having to defend his actions. Shrugging one shoulder, he tried again. "Running them out of town saves jail space for those who truly deserve it. Looters. Drunk drivers. Ax murderers."

His answer tugged a smile from her lips, and the tension riding on his shoulders slipped a notch. In a minute or two, he'd get a call—someone would have run their car into a ditch or spotted a downed wire—and have to respond. Until then, he couldn't think of anything he'd rather do than talk to Stephanie.

"How were things in Orlando?" he asked.

They stood on her lawn and discussed hurricanes and traffic until Brett felt his temperature drop to nearly normal. He had just started to hope his T-shirt might air dry before he climbed back into his cruiser when Stephanie switched subjects, choosing one that made him sweat for a whole new reason.

"Thanks for the sleeping bag. It was a good thing to have." She retrieved it from her car, which let him appreciate the way her hips moved beneath the clingy jersey. "I'll drop your sweatshirt off at the station once the power comes back. I want to wash it. I hope you don't mind that I wore it. I didn't have anything else—"

Brett's thoughts flew to an image of Stephanie in his

sweatshirt…and nothing else. The air around him grew warm. Forget the bottle of water. Where was a hose when you needed one?

"—appropriate," she finished.

He didn't have a hose, but the grass looked cool. He scuffed one foot through it, startling some kind of pink insect which flew off to the side.

"Oh! There it is!" Stephanie cried. She dropped to her hands and knees, running her fingers through the grass where the critter had landed.

"You like bugs?" he asked. They were a fact of life in Florida, but his last girlfriend had been scared to death by anything that possessed more legs than she did. As a result, Brett had been forced into pest control duty more often than he liked. A girl who didn't mind a few bugs would certainly be different. "You need some help?"

"No, that's okay. I lost…something." She stretched for the unidentified something, her top riding above a trim waistline. "And now I've found it."

Brett stared at a *very* nice inch of smooth, supple skin. He swallowed what felt like sand and felt the heat climb another degree. "Great." He managed not to sound too relieved. Getting down on all fours in the grass with her was not an option.

He offered her a hand up, intending to ask what she'd lost, but once the space in front of him filled with living, breathing Stephanie Bryant, his train of thought switched tracks. He had nearly forgotten how small she was. Her head and all those glorious curls didn't even reach the top of his shoulder. She peered up at him through incredibly blue eyes which, unless he was seriously misjudging the signals, were inviting him to take her into his arms. Uncertainty filled his head with static. It was such an unfamiliar feeling that he paused, wanting to be sure. When she did not wave a red flag, he leaned in slightly, forcing himself to go slow, giving her a chance to back away, praying she wouldn't.

The air between them crackled. A voice whispered in his ear.

"Lincoln, this is Dispatch. Those two yahoos are headed out on Highway 520. Merritt Island, Cocoa and points west have been alerted. They won't find work in the county. Good job, Brett."

Doris had a way of dousing a situation with cold water just when things were heating up nicely.

He tried to listen as she updated him on events throughout the town, but his attention kept wandering to Stephanie. The brunette had moved away and now stood with her cell phone pressed against one ear, her back to him. She kept talking after his call finished. Wondering who was on the other end of the line, he gathered tools that littered the ground beneath one of the windows, and waited until he heard her say, "I'll see you there in an hour."

Flipping the phone closed, Stephanie whirled to face him. "Sorry about that." She shrugged. "Work. I have to go into the office. Hey, did you find any glue in that toolbox? I broke a nail."

Brett shook his poor, confused head. If he needed proof she wasn't right for him, she had just given it. A girl had to be pretty self-centered to worry about a broken fingernail in the aftermath of a hurricane, didn't she? Hadn't he decided he was done with women like that?

"Time for both of us to get back to work," he announced. There would be no repeat of the almost-kiss. Not now. Not ever.

"All those ax murderers to chase?"

"Something like that. See you around." He was immune to the way her eyes sparkled. He was. So why did he have to force his feet toward the patrol car?

"Right. I've gotta run, too," she called.

She was in her car and pulling out of the driveway before he realized what was bothering him. Over one shoulder, he eyed the panels covering most of her windows. Heat and humidity would turn the inside of her house into a sweatbox. She'd need to strip down to her underwear in order to find any comfort at all.

The image of Stephanie Bryant, hot and sweaty and alone, was not one he wanted to carry with him until the power came back on.

Stifling a groan, he went back to the house and began removing her shutters.

Chapter Five

The guard trudged soundlessly through the hall on rubber-soled shoes. He passed one darkened office after another while Stephanie trailed behind, wishing the heels of her Jimmy Choo knockoffs wouldn't clatter so loudly against the marble floor. She could have worn sneakers and saved her aching arches for another day. It wasn't as if anyone would see her shoes during the telecom with Corporate.

The suit was another matter. Thanks to the latest in electronic gizmos, the bigwigs would get an eyeful of everything above her waist. From the megabucks they had invested in her, she knew they expected their newest director to be cool, calm and dressed to the nines, hurricanes and power outages notwithstanding. Thus, the quick change out of her sweats and into a suit in the ladies' room off the lobby. Shoes were just part of the package.

"Here you go, Ms. Bryant." The guard unlocked a door at the end of the hall.

Stephanie darted a quick look at his name tag. "Thank you, Paul."

The deference that came with her new title would take some getting used to. Not unlike her new office suite. A broad grin threatened to break across her face when she glanced past the empty receptionist's desk to the door of her very own spacious corner office.

"I'll be at the front desk if you need me. Will you be all right, Ms. Bryant?"

With backup generators powering the computers and air conditioners, she would be more than all right. "I'll be fine. Thanks for opening up for me, Paul."

She would get her own set of keys when she was formally introduced as the new director of human resources. Keys or not, she had work to do, and that work included research on the way the hurricane had impacted the company's biggest asset—its employees. Corporate had requested a 7:00 p.m. briefing, and she was determined to have all the answers to their questions by then.

Stephanie gave her escort a long look. Rain, wind, hail or hurricane, Space Tech's security force remained on guard, and the man had probably been on duty for days. It wouldn't hurt to gather a first-hand report from one of the company's own.

"Did you and your family come through the storm all right, Paul?" she asked.

He hesitated, his weight shifting from foot to foot. "Not exactly," he finally answered.

"Oh?"

"Our mobile home lost part of the roof. I'm just hoping it don't rain till I get enough time off to tarp it."

A hole in the roof of his trailer. Stephanie ran a hand through springy curls that refused taming without a blow-dryer and a flat iron. So what if she didn't have power? She lived in a solid house with an intact roof. She could tolerate a few curls.

"I'm sure the company values your loyalty, Paul, but you didn't want to take the day off?"

"We have a new baby in the house, ma'am. I can't afford a day without pay."

Stephanie noted folded arms and a firmly set jaw. Body language did not lie, and Paul's discomfort with the subject was easy to read. Reassurance rose in her throat, but she throttled it. He hadn't asked for any special favors. She would not offer empty promises. For now, she could only let him get back to work.

"Congratulations on the baby. Good luck with the roof," she said.

While he trudged back the way they had come, she crossed the anteroom, pausing at the doorway to her office to take in the green-and-gold patterned carpet beneath sand-colored walls. Company manuals filled two tall bookcases. Matching chairs and a conference table flanked the dark rosewood desk. Not the most impressive office she had ever seen, but it was hers. All hers. Now, if she could just keep it.

Corporate wanted assurance that everything was fine and dandy in the aftermath of the hurricane's near miss. "We don't expect this will require much action on our part," a senior VP cautioned.

Stephanie thought otherwise. Official reports—not those wildly speculative ones on the television—showed damage to one out of twenty homes and businesses throughout the county. Which meant, one out of twenty Space Tech employees could face the same awful choice Paul had made. The only way to help him, and others like him, would mean a temporary dip in the company's bottom line. Her research showed that assisting the employees with hurricane recovery would pay big dividends in the future, but was it worth the immediate risk to her career?

Weighing her answer, she walked to one of the picture

windows and looked out at the pine trees, palmettos and green grass. Sporadic lightning backlit a thick cloud bank that hovered on the horizon. Tomorrow's forecast called for rain.

She smoothed her collar, firmed her resolve, and joined the ongoing discussion at the appointed time.

Several hours of hard bargaining and compromise later, Stephanie logged out of the conference call. She propped her feet on the edge of her desk and leaned back. Toasting her success with a well-deserved swig of bottled water, she jiggled one foot until the charms dangling from her ankle strap clinked together. The sound made her grin.

Though they were only designer knockoffs, no one could tell her shoes from the real thing. And the other executives had taken her suggestions as seriously as if she were the real thing, too. Instead of a director so new to the job she didn't even have keys to her own office. So new to the area, she had to be told when to evacuate.

From evacuation, it was a simple jump to thoughts of Brett Lincoln and her mind played leapfrog. The way the hunky police officer had looked at her earlier brought steamy to a whole new level. But he hadn't kissed her. She would have bet money on that and lost.

Gladly, she insisted. Space Tech needed her. Her commitment to the welfare of its eight hundred local employees would leave no time for a relationship. If nothing else, today's events had proven that.

It had also added to her list of things to do before she headed home. After another sip of water, her feet hit the floor. A few keyboard clicks filled her computer screen with information. She picked up the phone and dialed.

"This is Stephanie Bryant in HR," she explained to the security supervisor when he answered. "I'd appreciate it if you called someone in to cover Paul's shift tomorrow."

She listened to the expected response. "Yes, I realize he doesn't have any vacation left. Give him the day off, with pay. I've already squared it with senior management. Charge it against this account." She rattled off a series of numbers tied to a pool of money the home office had grudgingly set aside.

The notifications would soon spread throughout the company. In a day, two at the most, Space Tech would reopen its doors and everyone with e-mail would know about the special leave plan. Those with significant, verifiable hurricane damage would be granted up to five days of *paid* personal time. Not only that, a special exemption would allow those who needed it to borrow from their retirement funds for repairs. The message was clear: the Space Tech family cared for its own.

She had seen to it. The ladder to success might have wobbled a bit, but she was still hanging on.

She eyed her office again. Without Brett's sleeping bag to curl up in, the floor would be harder than hard, so staying there wasn't an option. It was time to go home and pry off another storm shutter. She hadn't been able to accomplish the task earlier, so how she'd manage without daylight was perplexing, but manage she would. Hadn't she battled Corporate and won? Surely, she could take down a storm shutter or two. She powered down her laptop, shut off the lights and closed her office door.

STEPHANIE COULD not believe her luck. Dick and Sam *had* returned. They'd taken down her storm shutters and left them neatly propped against the wall next to the garage. Unfortunately, her luck did not extend to cell coverage she discovered when she tried to tell Brett he'd been wrong about the duo. She tapped her phone, but service was on the fritz again and the bars refused to appear. She flipped the phone closed. The chance to tease the cop could wait until morning. In the meantime, she would spend a delightfully cool evening in her new house, where sea breezes blew in through every window.

At work the next day, she delayed making the call until Paul's replacement escorted her through the halls. But by the time they reached her office, it was too late. Shrill phones rang on the other side of the door.

"Will the offices have electricity?" a caller asked.

"Yes," she said. "Power has been restored to all Space Tech buildings."

Not every business was so lucky, but the electric company had called for additional help, and contractors from all over the country were working around the clock to restore power. Top priority went to area hospitals and police stations, followed by a slowly expanding grid of homes and community services.

She dumped her laptop and briefcase onto the receptionist's desk before picking up another line. This caller had received an e-mail about extra vacation time and wanted to take it.

"What kind of storm damage do you have?" Stephanie asked. She grabbed a pad of paper and a pen, ready to take notes.

"None at all, thanks," answered the woman. "Our neighbors had a tree fall on their carport. Can you imagine? I don't know how I'd cope…"

The woman rambled on while Stephanie sipped coffee from Pat's Place. Many businesses and homes had backup generators. The convenience mart near her home was one of them, thank goodness. She shifted her briefcase to the floor. She doubted very much if she would make it as far as her office. She might not even get to eat breakfast. Her eyes flitted between a bag of doughnuts and the three blinking lights on the telephone console. Other callers were waiting. Stephanie broke in to explain that substantial, verifiable damage meant exactly that.

"I'm afraid you don't qualify," she said.

"Well, that hardly seems fair!" the caller huffed and hung up.

The whole help-the-Space-Tech-family thing had a few flaws, but every family had its share of kooks. You still invited them to Christmas dinner. Stephanie reached for the next in line.

"Will the day care be open?"

Ah, sanity. She took the caller's phone number and promised to check into it.

By midafternoon she had guided fifteen qualified employees—including a grateful Paul—through the maze of paperwork required for additional time off. She'd explained the application process to three besides the guard who needed to tap their retirement, returned the call about the day care facility—it would be open—and reassured practically everyone that business would return to normal at Space Tech the next day.

Some were happier with that information than others. She bit the inside of her cheek, struggling not to laugh at the woman who demanded permission to wear a halter top and shorts to work "because it's hot outside."

Of course, it was hot outside. It was summer. In Florida. Where eighty-seven signified a cold front and people broke out their winter woolens if the temperature dropped to seventy. But with massive air-conditioning units pumping chilly air throughout the complex, the dress code—unlike the halter top—would remain firmly in place.

The busy day high-stepped its way toward five o'clock when all calls would automatically reroute to the answering service. Though she loved the warm fuzzies that came with offering reassurance and help, Stephanie looked forward to a nice, long break before she tackled the glut of reports George Watson, their CEO, expected by morning. She rubbed elbows that felt raw from propping the phone to her face all day. Her suit was rumpled. Even the minimal makeup she wore had long since disappeared. So had the doughnut she'd scarfed with her morning coffee, and the second one she'd downed at lunch.

Her rumbling tummy demanded real food, making her wonder if any restaurants were open in the sections of town where power had been restored. And if they'd still be open by the time she headed home. She reached for the Yellow Pages, but lifted her head when a quiet thumping sounded in the hall. The tall, thin man who entered the office suite ignited a blaze of instant recognition and Stephanie gulped. She fought the urge to duck behind her computer screen.

Company founders came out of retirement only when things were truly messed up. And there was no doubt the man who stood on the other side of the secretary's desk was the company founder. The piercing gray eyes set in a long, narrow face, the shock of white hair, the shoulders held so straight their sharp angles could cut steel—his picture graced the inside cover of every company report.

Stephanie quickly smoothed her jacket. There was no smoothing her hair or her composure.

"Good afternoon, Mr. Sanders," she said rising to greet him. Thinking the curt nod and accompanying grimace he shot her way were bad omens, she stiffened. Her hands dropped to her sides, her fingers gripped the edge of the desk and curled under it.

He crossed his own gnarled hands atop a hand-carved cane tall enough to use without stooping. "Where's your boss?" he demanded, his voice gruff.

"I—" Her glance followed his to her darkened office. While she could claim the boss had never arrived, what would that make her? The receptionist? It was probably the position she'd land in if she missed a rung on the corporate ladder, but why give him ideas? She cleared her throat.

"I'm Stephanie Bryant," she said. "I am the boss."

"So." Unhappy eyes ran the length of her. "It was your suggestion to create an emergency fund from company profits?"

Though her posture would never be as straight as his, Stephanie pulled herself erect, looked the company founder straight between the collarbones and gave him the textbook answer.

"Yes. I estimate increased employee retention and decreased turnover at ten percent. As you know, both of those numbers significantly impact profits—"

The pragmatic approach had worked with Corporate. It didn't go over well with Mr. Sanders. His frosty look sent a chill down Stephanie's spine and she wrapped up quickly.

"Over the long term, that is."

"Very generous of you. Especially with my money." The left side of his mouth shifted into a brief scowl. When it straightened, he peered down over the tall desk separating them. "Why are you working here?" he demanded.

"I'm sorry?" Did he mean here, at Space Tech? Or, here, at this desk? If his glare was any indication, she wouldn't be at either long.

"Why is my director of human resources sitting at her secretary's desk and not in her office?"

Stephanie practically heard the soft chime of the elevator descending all the way to the basement. She considered making something up, something practical, something straight out of an economics textbook, but she knew it wouldn't be the truth. If her career was going to go splat, she owed herself that much. The truth.

"I never made it that far. We had a lot of calls, and the phone in my office doesn't have enough lines to handle them."

"That's because your predecessor avoided such work. He felt direct communication with our employees was better left to their managers."

Her predecessor. One day the man had been sitting in this office. The next, all trace of him had vanished. His abrupt departure had triggered her promotion, one she had hoped to keep.

"My philosophy is more…hands-on. I could have ignored the phones, but our employees needed reassurance. Giving it to them made all of us feel better." Hearing herself, Stephanie thought she might gag. She'd been around long enough to realize that *touchy-feely* didn't earn any Brownie points with the corporate mucky-mucks.

"I take it some of our employees required a bit of hand-holding?"

Had she really seen his lips curve? Everyone knew John Sanders never smiled, but for a second there she would have sworn…

"You could say that. I think I spoke with every one of them. Some of them twice."

The harsh lines around the founder's face dissolved. "As well you should, my dear. As well you should. Never lose sight of the fact that our employees are people and people have problems. When we can, we want to help them."

Stephanie blinked to hide her shock. If she wasn't

mistaken, John Sanders had just applied the brakes to her free-falling career.

"Now, did you consider a fundraiser?" he continued. "Perhaps an old-fashioned carnival?"

Thinking Corporate would consider the idea too "girly," she hadn't suggested it. She had, however, calculated the risks. Any number of factors—inclement weather, poor turnout, insurance rates—could cause such an event to lose money. "If we don't deplete the emergency fund, we'll throw a back-to-normal barbecue in a month or two."

Nodding, John Sanders scanned the surface of the desk where her laptop sat open. "And I suppose George wants a million and one reports? Don't stay here until they're done tonight."

That sounded an awful lot like an order. "No?" she asked.

"There will be enough chaos tomorrow without adding an exhausted HR director into the mix. Go home. Have a nice dinner. Get some rest. You'll need it."

Since arguing with the company founder wouldn't enhance her career, she clamped her mouth shut before it could disagree. The reports couldn't be ignored altogether, but a laptop made the work portable.

"I'll walk out with you," she said.

A nice, long break was just what the doctor, er, company founder, had ordered. The warm fuzzies were all her own. She gathered up her things.

The sun was a huge orange ball sinking behind streaks of gold cloud when she pulled out of the parking lot at Petty's. Like many businesses on the mainland, the upscale butcher shop was back in business, and a sampling of gourmet takeout now rested in a heavy paper bag on the floorboard beside her. Driving across the causeway, Stephanie inhaled deeply. The buttery smell of garlic rolls competed with the briny tang of the ocean. Both were so appealing she couldn't decide which one she liked best.

All in all, it had been a good day. Hard work, but no more than she'd expected. She had been able to help several Space Tech employees. And any day you made friends with the company founder, that was a good day, indeed.

With the power still out for most of the barrier islands, intersections had become four-way stops. As she slowed to wait her turn at one, Stephanie eyed a tall drift of wind-blown sand that narrowed the road. Traffic cleared, and she was halfway through the intersection when another car barreled up behind her.

"Hey! Watch out!" she protested as a fast-moving, black convertible drew even. The drift was right in front of her. With a split second to choose between getting sideswiped or plowing into sand, she chose the sand.

Mired to its hubcaps, her car rocked to an immediate stop.

BRETT WATCHED the traffic move in an orderly fashion through the intersection until he realized his heart wasn't in the job.

Normally, he loved the first few days after a big blow. Residents of the small town banded together. They held neighborhood cookouts so the meat in their freezers would not go to waste. They broke out their chain saws and cleared debris from each other's driveways. They cut "the other guy" some slack. Yes, there were a few losers, such as Dick and his pal Sam, con artists who tried to take advantage. But they were easy to spot, and nearly as easy to deal with. And sure, later—by week's end if Florida Power and Light didn't get the electric restored—all that newfound camaraderie would fray. But the first few days after a hurricane were all wine and roses. Sort of like a honeymoon.

Wine and roses and...who? He pictured a woman dressed in a long white gown, dark curls spilling over bare shoulders as she reclined against a thousand pillows on a wide canopied bed. The image stirred a yearning so deep and unexpected it rattled him.

What the...? He didn't think about honeymoons. Or getting married, for that matter. Certainly not to someone he'd barely met, even if the mere sight of her stirred him to pick up a sword and shield and slay all her dragons. Brett slugged back coffee and forced himself into an upright and uncomfortable position. He was suffering from sleep deprivation, that had to be the problem. Show him a guy whose thoughts didn't wander after seventy-two hours of round-the-clock duty, and he'd show you a guy who...

His head and his focus snapped to attention when a black convertible sped past his patrol car in a horn-blowing blare. Spewing sand and grit, the car made the turn off the causeway onto the main beachside road without even slowing down. Brett studied the intersection. No collisions. No cars off the road. Everyone startled, but okay. He hit his lights and siren, speaking into his mike, his car in motion before the sand settled back onto the asphalt.

"Dispatch, this is Lincoln. In pursuit of a black Mustang convertible, license unknown. Southbound from State Road 520 on A1A."

Doris's voice was all business. "Lincoln, this is Dispatch. Break off at Cocoa Isles Boulevard. I say again. Break off pursuit of black Mustang at Cocoa Isles. Hand off to Davis and Smith."

"Roger that, Dispatch." He was no slouch, but Jake Davis was the finest police officer on the force. He'd have the reckless driver tested for alcohol and spread-eagled before his tires quit spinning.

Brett allowed himself a tight smile. One more block, and he'd relinquish the chase into Jake's good hands.

It was one too many.

The Mustang blasted through another crossroad. This time cars careened out of its path. One—a familiar navy sedan—swung to the side, throwing up a plume of sand as it went. The car rocked to a stop, its nose buried in a drifting dune.

Recognition and denial warred within him as Brett's heart did a slow roll. The one person he wanted to protect above all others was in that car.

"It can't be," he whispered.

He was out of his unit, his feet pounding against the pavement. At least, he thought his feet were pounding. Something was, but he wasn't making any progress in his race to the sedan. It took an eternity to cover the fifty feet from his car to hers. Through a side window he saw a spill of dark curls. He wrenched the door open, his eyes assessing the scene, his thoughts rushing.

Stephanie slumped, motionless, across the steering wheel. Brett froze, unable to breathe, until her hand moved. He heard a soft moan escape her lips.

"Alive," he whispered. "Thank heaven."

He took a half sip of air when Stephanie pushed away from the steering wheel and struggled to straighten herself. She tipped to one side, taking his heart right along with her. Frightening possibilities—seizure, whiplash, internal bleeding—filled his head.

Before he could help her, she sat up, dragging a bag with a familiar logo out of the footwell on the passenger side. She peered into the sack.

"Oh, thank goodness," she exclaimed. "Nothing's broken."

Nothing but my head, Brett thought. *I should have it examined.*

His heart slowly slipped down his throat and back into his chest where it belonged. It pumped hard enough to make his breath sound harsh as he stared down at Stephanie. "You all right?" he asked.

She looked…fine. The large paper bag blocked his view of her waist and hips but, judging from the way she swung her feet from the car, all working parts were in good order.

"Don't worry about me."

She sounded a little out of breath. That could be the excitement or she could be injured. She could have banged into the steering wheel and hurt…something. Brett zeroed in on her chest.

"The guy who ran me off the road. He's the one you need to worry about."

He jerked his focus up where it belonged before he got caught staring and spoke. "He kept on going. Didn't stop."

Communication chattered through his earpiece. Jake had pulled the Mustang over and was even now reading the driver his rights. Joining them made no sense and, besides, he had something more important to tend to. Brett switched his radio off.

"Are you just going to let him speed on down the road until somebody gets hurt? Go after him. I'm fine."

She was fine? Irritated was more like it. Maybe she *had* banged her head.

"Let's just make sure you're all right first," he said. "Any pain? Did you black out? Lose consciousness?" It was hard to tell if a person's pupils were dilated when eyes narrowed the way Stephanie's did.

"I told you, I'm not hurt. I wasn't going that fast. Look," she gestured. "The air bag didn't even deploy."

Brett checked the dashboard for damage and saw none. No drape of white plastic over the steering wheel. No cracks in the windshield. Nothing.

Maybe he was overreacting a bit. Like he had the time one of Tom's girls had tangled with a jellyfish at the beach. The toddler's tears had brought him to his knees, and he had practically dialed 911 before Mary doused the tiny welt with meat tenderizer. The baby's tears had dried in an instant. Not so Tom and Mary's teasing—that had gone on for months. He knew he had overreacted then because the girls meant so much to him. But why was his normally un-flappable heart chugging along like a runaway train now? The reason frowned up at him.

"Do you think you can stand?" he asked her.

"Of course."

Wanting, needing to help, he reached for her arm, but ended up holding the sack Stephanie thrust into his out-stretched hand.

"I can manage," she proclaimed.

Her narrow skirt would make maneuvering a struggle under normal circumstances. Toss in a pair of shoes better designed for a runway in Paris than the beach, and her balance was bound to be skewed. But Brett had surfed often enough to get out of the water when the sharks were biting. He stepped back to give her room, easing into a crouch as he freed his hands of her grocery bag.

To her credit, she made it practically upright before pencil-thin heels tunneled into the loose sand. With an un-ladylike, "Awk!" she tumbled backward. Brett lunged, managing to wrap his arms around her before she hit the car. He tugged her to him just as his own feet found the edge of the roadway and slipped off. If he'd been any shorter or less solid, they both might have spilled onto the ground, but he regained his footing quickly. It would take a lot more than ninety pounds of girl and a little crumbled asphalt to bring him down.

Or maybe not…

His arms filled with warm, breathing Stephanie Bryant. The heady scent of her perfume found its way straight into his brain where it purged all thoughts except how much he wanted her in his life. As he realized he had her right where he'd wanted her since the moment she'd opened her front door, need tugged across his hips, surged into his center and headed south.

His reaction was so immediate and so startlingly obvious that he reared back. His hands skimmed upward over soft curves to her shoulders and he forced his elbows straight until he held her at arm's length. He searched her face, hoping he hadn't scared her to death. As for himself, he was already halfway there.

Chapter Six

Stephanie felt herself falling backward, and just had time to realize her head was inches from a nasty blow when Brett's strong arms swept her away from harm.

Thank goodness he'd caught her in time. This rescue—unlike some of the others—was real enough. So why did she suspect she had merely traded one danger for another? She didn't have an answer for that question, but she knew what she wanted. She wanted to rest her cheek against Brett's crisp khaki shirt and press her head to his wide chest. She wanted to listen to the steady beat of his heart. She'd grabbed for him as she fell, and now her hands seemed reluctant to leave his narrow hips while his fingers firmly gripped her waist. He held her as if he would never let her go and she leaned into him, daring herself to want the same thing. A world of possibilities was just opening up when he jerked back as if she was kryptonite.

"Jeez. Sorry," he mumbled. "I didn't mean to crush you like that."

If she could have, she would have scratched her head where confusion had moved in and set up housekeeping. Instead, she sought firmer footing on the pavement and reached for his hand.

"Thanks," she said. "I mean it."

"Just doing my job."

Warmth radiated from him, sending a delicious shiver through her as his large hand engulfed her smaller one. Her thoughts evaporated like morning dew when the sun came up. The urge to move into his arms again was strong but she resisted, struggling to remember something that was just out of her grasp. She knew it was something important, but she couldn't quite...

She retrieved her hand and took a step back.

Oh, yeah. It was a bad idea to start a relationship the same week she started her dream job. Though at the moment, it was difficult to remember why.

She'd have to think about that later, after her hand stopped tingling.

"So, what about the other guy?" she asked. "The one who ran me off the road. Did he get away?"

Brett angled his chin to a spot farther down the beach where blue lights flashed brightly against the dark sky. His voice did not invite discussion when he said, "They got him. He's earned a night's stay in lockup."

"Guess I'll be going, then. Think I can get my car back on the road?" She slipped her feet free of the infernal sandals and bent down to pick them up. When he didn't answer, she shot the tall cop a questioning glance that caught him staring into the darkness where waves crashed on the shore behind the dunes.

"Brett?"

He blinked, coming back from wherever he'd gone. His attention shifted to her car. Sand just reached the front hubcaps. The back wheels were still angled out onto the shoulder. As she imagined, the front end barely touched the encroaching dune. Brett slipped behind the wheel and backed the car onto the pavement with apparent ease.

"I'd have someone look it over, especially that air bag, if it were mine. But the brakes feel okay. Steering, too. I can follow you home if you'd like. Make sure you get there safely."

Now that they weren't touching, she could almost think rationally again. Brett Lincoln made a great knight on a white horse, but she didn't want a man in her life. Not even one who rode to her rescue at the slightest provocation.

She moved her head firmly from side to side. "I'm sure that's not necessary. Like you said, everything is working. And it's only a short way home."

She stepped toward the car where he held the door while she pulled her shoes back on. As she swung into the seat, he lingered at her window.

"How's the house? You get enough air with the shutters off?"

The question brought her head around. "How did you know about the shutters?" He refused to meet her eyes as she frowned up at him. "You took them down?"

When he nodded, her confusion unpacked its bags and settled in for a long stay. "I thought Dick and his buddy came back and finished the job."

Brett made a chuffing noise. "The only job those jokers were interested in was how much money they could take you for. I know that sounds harsh, but it's the way these guys work."

"So, why did you…"

"Dispatch wanted me to keep an eye out for them in case they circled around after you left. I figured I might as well make myself useful."

Useful, indeed. The work must have taken hours and it

was so far beyond the call of duty she couldn't let it go unchallenged. "It's too much, Brett. I can't accept—"

Despite the darkness, she saw his blue eyes sparkle. "You want me to rehang your shutters?"

"Well, no…" she began. The closed-up house would be an oven until the power came back on.

"Consider it a welcome gift, then. I— Hey. Hold on."

He ducked away from her window before her protests continued. She watched him in the rearview mirror as he trudged through the sand to retrieve something from the ground.

"We nearly forgot your bag," he said.

The sack of groceries he settled on her backseat offered a tangible way to say thanks. "What time does your shift end?" she asked.

"We're on 24/7 till all the hurricane mess gets sorted out, but I have a dinner break coming up. Do you need something?"

She laughed. "You absolutely, positively cannot do one more thing for me. I'll never be able to repay you as it is." Not wanting to mislead him, she added, "And I'm not going to try."

"That doesn't seem fair," he grumbled with a smile that let her know he was joking.

"I'll never eat all the food I bought at the market. It seems a shame to let an excellent meal go to waste. Why don't you come over and we'll have supper."

As Stephanie pulled onto the road, she told herself not to read too much into Brett's ready acceptance. Supper, that's all it was. Supper and a chance to throw some roadblocks in the path of what she could not deny was a growing attraction. So far, it was mostly physical, and she needed to keep it that way. If they spent some time together, she was certain their sexual attraction would fade in the face of all their differences. After all, he was a macho cop, determined to argue with practically every word that came out of her mouth, while she was all about coopera- tion and her career.

Her job might not keep her warm at night, but heat wasn't exactly a problem in Florida...in the sum- mer...with no air-conditioning. The sky glowed over the distant mainland where electricity was quickly being restored. Not so in Cocoa Beach or the rest of the barrier islands. From Cape Canaveral to the Sebastian Inlet, *When do we get power?* was the question on the lips of everyone from the gas station attendant who could not pump gas to the convenience store owner who gave away the contents of his freezers rather than see the food go to waste.

Stephanie wanted the miracle of electricity as much as anybody else. She especially longed to hear the soothing crash of waves on the beach again. From her driveway, she listened to machines that whined like a hundred airplanes revving for takeoff. The generators belonging to her more hurricane-savvy neighbors drowned out all other sound.

She still had the sky, though. A crescent moon and a billion stars normally hidden by the glare of city lights lit her way to the front door where she fumbled her key into the lock. Inside, black heat ruled.

She lugged her bags, briefcase and laptop to the kitchen counter. The rustle of plastic and paper bags seemed un- naturally loud without the usual dampening effect of electric appliances. Feeling for the flashlight and portable radio, she kicked off her heels and listened to them skid into a corner before she raced through the house, throwing open all the windows. A cool ocean breeze rushed through the screens. It was exactly what she had asked for, though it threatened to snuff out the thick, white candles she lit in place of lamps.

Inviting Brett to dinner already had her in a sweat, but the addition of heat and humidity drove her into the shower. With the only choice being cold water or more cold water, she was under the spray and out again almost before the chill bumps formed.

"What to Wear When Serving Post-Hurricane Takeout" might make a nice addition to her evacuation class, she decided as she shifted impatiently in front of her closet. Her flashlight played over a dizzying array of clothes designed to fit the Florida lifestyle. In her mind they clung too tightly, plunged too low or didn't cover enough of her midsection. They would do nothing for the roadblocks she intended to erect between her and a certain cop. With a sigh, she chose a flippy print, hoping the stretchy yellow crop top she wore with it turned the sheer blouse into something halfway decent. Drab Bermuda shorts and scuffs completed her outfit without adding to its allure.

She pushed damp curls from her face and decided to forego her usual makeup, as well. The sticky heat would only make it run, but lipstick was another matter. Lipstick was like underwear. It didn't take much—just a little dab— but you didn't walk around without it. She had just finished gliding the merest shimmer around her mouth when she heard a knock at the front door. Her hand tightened on the small tube.

What had she been thinking, inviting a Greek god to dinner?

Maybe she hadn't been thinking. Maybe it wasn't a good idea to rush around in air as thick and hot as a sauna's. That was how people got heatstroke, wasn't it? She paused, thinking of all the ways and places she'd like Brett to stroke until a second rap on the door interrupted a very pleasant daydream. She shook her head.

There would be no hanky-panky with Brett Lincoln. He was physically attractive, no doubt, and he had this noble habit of being Johnny-on-the-spot at the first sign of trouble. Problem was, she didn't need Johnny, or his spot—thank you very much. Not when her goal was to prove how well she could manage herself, her people and her company on her own. No, she wanted Brett in her world as much as she wanted a rash.

But like it or not, he *was* in her world. And he made her itch all over.

BRETT'S HEAD dipped forward just as his dream started to get interesting. He jolted awake.

"Only a dream," he muttered.

He was alone in his squad car, just as he had been ten minutes earlier when he turned off the ignition key. Endless back-to-back shifts were having their way with him and the catnap had crept up unannounced. If there was one good thing about not having his way with Stephanie tonight, that was it—he would probably fall asleep and miss all the fun. Before he could drift off again and miss the evening altogether, Brett levered himself from the car and made his way to the front door.

At first glance, the outfit she wore to greet him was disappointingly modest, but Brett quickly reminded himself that he wasn't there to check her out. He already knew the sassy brunette turned him on. What he needed now was to find out more about the girl who owned the phenomenal bod before his libido drove him into a wall.

As he followed her to the kitchen, his fog-shrouded

brain stirred with an altogether different kind of hunger. He breathed in the smoky scent of grilled chicken, the tang of citrus. Pineapple tickled his nose with its tart smell. There were sharp spices nearby, and a whiff of garlic floated in the air. He darted a look from Stephanie to the heaping dish she set before him. Three days of vending machine fare left him uncertain which to devour first, so he took his cue from the petite brunette. His fork plunged to the plate.

"So, Brett, how long have you lived here?" Stephanie asked a short while later.

"I'm a Florida cracker," he answered between bites. "That's what they call us natives. Except for a stint in the Marines and college, I've lived here all my life."

"You didn't want to travel, see the world?" Her brows, which hiked whenever something confused or upset her, rose a tad.

"I saw enough of it in the Marines to know people are pretty much the same no matter where you go. Good guys are good. Bad guys are bad. The rest is just window dressing."

"Officer Lincoln!" Stephanie grabbed her heart and leaned back, laughing. "Do I detect a touch of cynicism?"

He ignored the playful sparkle in her eyes to shrug an answer. "I fight it every day," he said. "Usually, it wins." His image of public service had tarnished faster than his shiny gold badge.

Instantly, she sobered. "I've heard that policemen make great cynics. You think it's part of the job?"

He shoveled in a forkful of pasta salad and bit into something that filled his mouth with a burst of sharp flavor. The taste brought him all the way awake as he studied the figure seated across the table. There was nothing judgmental in the even tone, or in the way she cocked her head to one side. Brett catalogued the kindness and sympathy that darkened Stephanie's eyes. They might wind up in bed together—would, if the choice were his to make—but she wasn't part of his world. Not yet. He had nothing to lose by being honest.

"It's a lot more common than you think," he said.

"It is? Tell me, what made you choose law enforcement in the first place?"

"The same things as the rest of the force. Most of us go into police work thinking we'll make a difference. We're going to help Joe Citizen and get the bad guys off the street. But you rarely see Joe Citizen. Unless you write him a speeding ticket—which he does not appreciate—or someone robs him, he doesn't need your help, and he doesn't want you dropping in for a friendly chat in case you discover the marijuana growing in his backyard. So, instead, you spend all your time chasing the bad guys. And when you catch them, they're back on the streets doing whatever got them in trouble to begin with before you finish the paperwork."

He stopped to take a breath. What had gotten into him? He never talked about this kind of stuff, had never discussed it with anyone he'd dated. Yet here he was, confessing his deepest secrets to a girl he barely knew well enough to give his name, rank and serial number. What would it be like to have someone he could share such feelings with every day?

At that scary thought, he ordered his mouth closed and told it not to say another word.

"Yeah, I'm cynical. A lot of the guys on the force are. People on the outside don't understand that, so we stick together."

His mouth was a traitor. To keep it quiet, he stuffed a whole pillow of ravioli into it.

"You know I'm new to the area." Stephanie brightened as if he hadn't just poured his heart and soul onto her kitchen table. "Before the storm, I saw a bunch of boats in the neighborhood. That must be fun—out on the water, the wind in your hair, the spray in your face." She tossed her head and fluffed her curls the way the wind might blow them. "You ever do that? Take a girl out on your boat?"

As much as he relished the chance to see Stephanie's curvy body in a string bikini, annoyance lanced through him as the conversation veered into shallow waters.

"I don't own a boat," he said. "Or skis. When I'm not at work, I hang out with the other guys on the force."

"You live in Florida and you don't take advantage of it?" A sad disbelief glistened in her blue eyes. "You don't lie out on the beach? You don't go water-skiing? Or fishing?"

When she put it that way, it made him sound pretty dull. "I surfed when I was a kid. And I used to do a little fly fishing now and again, but work's kept me too busy lately."

"Oh. That's too bad." She nibbled on a bacon-wrapped date and said nothing more until the pit lay on her plate and she had picked up a garlic roll. She began to shred it. "You ought to think about taking that back up," she said.

Crumbs mounded onto her plate. Brett didn't have any idea what she was talking about and let his expression say as much.

"Fly fishing. You should do more of it. Having an outside interest is one of the keys to overcoming job burnout. Another is spending time with people besides your co-workers. And physical activity—working out, running, playing basketball, joining a softball team—it all helps."

It was a good thing he had stopped eating because his jaw dropped open. Misjudging this girl was turning into a bad habit.

"What?" he managed.

She continued turning the garlic roll into a million tiny pieces.

"You're a cynic," she said without glancing up from her plate. "You weren't one when you joined the force. You became a cop because you wanted to help people. But you're in a high-stress job. Your work puts you in constant contact with the worst elements of society. People Are Safe never makes the headlines, so you rarely see the rewards. The very nature of your work fosters an us-against-the-world attitude. Face it, Brett."

She dropped what was left of the roll onto her plate and pinned him with a look that was pure challenge.

"You're walking the job-burnout line. If you don't make changes to correct it, you'll end up just as jaded and disillusioned as the old-timers in your department. You know them, don't you? Who taught you the ropes of police work?"

"Jake," he said. "Jake is the best training officer I've ever known."

"Let me guess. He comes down hard on the people he arrests. And he never cuts—what were your words? Joe Citizen? He never cuts JC any slack. He's at least twenty pounds overweight. Divorced. Antisocial, except around other cops. He drinks too much."

Brett blinked. Her description had nailed his old partner. "Where did you two meet?"

"We haven't." Stephanie shrugged. "What I described is classic job burnout. In HR, we see it every day. Engineers who build their lives around their work. Corporate executives who tire of the rat race. Most of what we know, and how to fix it, we learned from studying cops. Their burnout rate is one of the highest."

She was wrong about him and Jake. They'd seen more

than their share of hard cases, but burnout? The idea was laughable. He was still marshaling his thoughts, determined to show how wrong she was, when she abandoned the battlefield without giving him a chance to prove he had the superior argument.

"So, we were talking about travel. And you said it was all window dressing. What'd you mean by that?"

He weighed answers while he stirred his fork through the remains of pasta salad, searching for another of those tasty olives. So what if she had pegged him as a cynical cop? His opinion of sightseeing was sure to raise her hackles further than her eyebrows would stretch, but she deserved it after the way she'd slammed his job.

"Churches here don't look anything like the mosques in Tehran," he said, "but they're all places of worship. The Grand Canyon was caused by a river and the Vredefort Dome is a meteor strike, but they're both big holes in the ground. A hotel in Brussels offers the same lousy mattresses as one in Vegas."

Sure enough, that brought her brows to full attention. He would have laughed at the surprised "oh" her mouth formed if it didn't look so kissable.

"But travel is more than that, isn't it? It's the Alps and Angel Falls and an archipelago in the South Pacific."

One mountain looked pretty much like any other in his book, but her voice was infectious. The endearing way her cheeks flushed when something excited her made him wonder if seeing the world through *her* eyes would make a difference.

He threw down a challenge. "If you like travel so much, why aren't you out seeing the world?"

"I plan to." She nodded. "I want to see it all." She chose another garlic roll from the pile on the table. Using it as a pointer, she traced an invisible map through the air. "Everything from the Sistine Chapel and Buckingham Palace to the Taj Mahal and the Pyramids." Her voice faltered. "I just, you know, can't yet."

The way the light in her eyes dimmed caught his immediate attention. "Yeah?" She lived in a house on the beach. She had no roots, no husband, no children to tie her down. She didn't even own a cat, a decided plus in his book. "What's stopping you?"

"A couple of things." She speared a bit of fresh mozzarella and tomato. Her laden fork traced circles over the plate. "Money, for one. Space Tech has a terrific corporate training program but they don't pay much to start. Back in Ohio, I even lived with my parents." She flashed a grin at his pained expression. "This assignment is my first big test. If I succeed, my next position will be bigger and more challenging. Since I only have a year to prove they made the right decision by giving me this shot, I owe them every minute of my time. For a year. At least."

He heard the warning in her words while his eyes traveled the granite counters and tile floors. A year, and she'd be moving on to greener pastures leaving him to say he knew her when. Rather than dwelling on that disturbing thought, he studied the overhead fan where wide paddles turned lazily, powered by the ocean breeze. He gestured toward the open sliding glass door.

"This is a great place," he said. "I was afraid the previous owners, the Hensons, might tear it down. I was glad when they decided to rebuild."

She stopped nibbling on the tomato wedge and lowered her fork. "Why would they even consider it?"

Brett shrugged. He didn't have anything more to tell her than what everyone else knew.

"Two years ago, Tropical Storm Wanda stalled right on top of us. She wasn't as strong as a hurricane, but she did some serious damage. A tree, a palm if I remember right, smashed straight through this roof. By the time the Hensons returned from their son's house up north, rain had drenched the walls and carpets. Mildew and mold ruined whatever the water didn't. They gutted the house. Replaced everything from the roof to the floor tiles," he explained.

When she didn't respond, he studied the mix of shock and surprise that crept over her face. "You didn't know any of this? It's pretty much common knowledge around here."

"My real estate agent never said a word," Stephanie murmured. "In fact, she practically boasted that the geography of this area prevented hurricanes from coming ashore."

"Real estate agent? Huh!" Experience with a particular blonde left him wary of the profession. "Meteorologists define landfall as the point where the center of the storm, the eye, comes ashore. But the storms extend out for hundreds of miles. So a miss, even a not-so-near miss, can do a lot of damage. Your agent didn't exactly lie—we've never taken a direct hit, at least not from a full-fledged hurricane. But we have seen our share of wrecked homes and businesses. We had quite a bit of damage from Hurricane Arlene, too. "

"One in twenty businesses and homes," she said.

He caught Stephanie staring at the ceiling as if she expected to see a tree trunk plunge through it.

"Relax," he told her. "Your roof is solid."

Intending to give the barest reassuring squeeze and be back on his side of the table before she knew he was coming, he placed his hand over her smaller one. But the instant they touched, his fingers slipped between hers and somehow tangled there. Heat flew up his arm as his thumb rubbed the length of her index finger. The warmth gathered until his chest filled with it, the overflow spilling into a wave that swept all the way down to his heels.

"Until we take a direct hit," she said. Still staring at the ceiling, she ran the tip of her tongue across her upper lip.

One push. One little push. That's all it would take to scare her straight back to Ohio and out of his life. All he had to do was to agree with her.

"It will never happen," he said firmly.

HE WAS HER OPPOSITE in every way that counted, a disillusioned cop who resented her advice and disagreed with her view of the world. He might look like a Greek god, but she didn't need, or want, anyone rushing to her rescue, even if he was intelligent and honest. Still, she couldn't deny how safe and protected he made her feel.

When Stephanie meant to pull her fingers from beneath Brett's grip, the order fizzled somewhere between her brain and her arm. She licked her lips and reached for her water glass.

Her body might want him, but she was smarter than that. Brett Lincoln was too big a complication, too big a risk. His presence threatened years of hard work and sacrifice. She knew it, and she was in control.

He had to go. It really was that simple. She would rid her life of him and she would start right here, right now. As soon as she could force her reluctant body to follow her lead, she would do it.

She rose abruptly, the move catching her rebellious hand so unaware it slipped free. She shook her fingers, trying to ease the sensation of his touch. No luck. Her body buzzed so much it sent words leaping from her mouth in a staccato stream.

"Thanks-for-coming-and-for-the-windows-and-for-every-thing-else-but-I-have-a-big-day-tomorrow-and-it's-time-to-go."

Throwing a sidelong glance his way, she saw Brett sitting in shell-shocked silence. She could not fault his dazed look. She had just rung the bell on their budding re-lationship and she had not even cushioned the blow. She hated to be harsh, but it was too late to change her mind. Irritated, with herself as much as with the situation, she stalked across the kitchen to stuff an armload of paper plates and takeout containers beneath the trash can's lid. She spun, intending to gather the rest of the debris…and collided with a muscular chest. She would have lost her balance for the second time that evening except for Brett's hands. His steady grip found her waist, kept her upright and shot scorching flames through her midsection.

She tipped her head at his murmured apology, hesitat-ing at the way candlelight reflected in his blue eyes. The sight reminded her of Icarus and the sun, and she recog-nized the danger in flying too close. She leaned back to catch her breath, but knew she was doomed the second his spicy, woodsy scent filled her. She flowed into his arms.

An indescribable thrill shot through her as he bent to press his full lips to her own. The feeling was so unexpect-edly delicious she gasped, her lips barely parting. It was all the permission he needed to slip between them.

The move sent waves of shocked pleasure rolling to her center. She trembled beneath his touch as his fingers trailed along her waist. Her hands found his back where they clenched and kneaded. He drew her to him. At the first brush of her breasts against his chest he uttered a groan that she felt all the way down to her toes. His hands slipped around to her back, massaging the small sensitive hollows just below her waist, and he urged her even closer. She moaned softly as an exquisite pressure began to build beneath his caress. The air hummed with the intensity of their embrace.

But when things started to vibrate, Stephanie's eyes flew open.

Trying to get her bearings under the glaringly bright lights of a fully electrified kitchen, she narrowed in on the refrigerator's noisy buzz. From the living room, the television blared static. Below one kitchen window came a loud roar as the air conditioner shook itself into action.

Musty air poured out of the overhead vent and Stephanie went cold. What had she been doing with the man she had practically thrown out of her house? Was she insane? The same thoughts must have occurred to Brett because their hands dropped simultaneously. She felt mortification stain her cheeks and stepped back, reaching instinctively for the safety and solidity of the kitchen counter. Taking an unsteady breath, she looked for some way to put needed distance between them without swinging the pendulum all the way from firebrand to ice queen.

Her gesture swept the room. "Did we do that?" she asked.

Lame by any standards, the joke broke the tension. Brett smiled, his eyes crinkling.

"It was bound to happen," he said. A pause, then, "I have to go." He nodded toward her front door and, beyond it, the city. "With the power back on, there are bound to be problems. I'll, uh, I'll call you."

"About that, um…" Her fingertips grazed his forearm and felt only skin. The fire had burned itself out. She took a deep breath and made the only sensible choice. "With the rest of the employees reporting to work tomorrow and getting settled in the new job and all, I'll be insanely busy for the next few weeks, so, um—"

"Don't call me, I'll call you?" he finished for her.

"Yeah. Something like that." She forced her eyes to meet his while, for once, her thoughts begged for an argument.

"Okay by me." His walk to her front door defined non-chalance. "Thanks for dinner," he called before disappearing into the night. Seconds later, she heard an engine rev and tires pull away from her curb.

It was the right thing to do, she told herself. No matter how much her body craved his touch, there was no room in her immediate future for a tall, broad-shouldered cop who rode to her rescue every time she had a hangnail. Especially if he didn't care. Which he must not, considering how easily he'd walked away.

Once the door was locked behind him, the windows closed and the thermostat lowered to bone-chill, she headed for the shower. Their kiss might have meant nothing to Brett, but she still smoldered. Turning the tap on full force, she realized it would take hours for the hot water heater to recharge.

She would need every one of them.

Chapter Seven

Stephanie's work phone rang twenty, sometimes thirty, times a day. Which made for a lot of sipped air and bruised feelings whenever the display showed a number other than Brett's. Which it had done far longer than she'd thought he could possibly hold out. Never mind that she had told him not to call. She couldn't take much more of his cold shoulder. She could handle broad shoulders, though. Especially Brett's, which were broad enough and strong enough to— Her breath hitched when the phone rang, but she refused to look up from the report she was finalizing

When the phone buzzed again, she swallowed frustration at the unfamiliar number on her Caller ID and picked up.

"Hello. This is Stephanie Bryant."

"Stephanie, it's Mary Jenkins. You may not remember me, but…"

But she made a point of remembering names and faces. In the moment before she joined the conversation, she flipped through the pertinent facts. Mary was married to Tom. Tom's best friend was on the CBPD.

"Of course I remember you, Mary. How are you? How are the girls? And Tom?" Maybe he could ask his friend to ask Brett to— Yeah, and, like, high school was soooo yesterday.

"Fine. We're all fine. I hope it's okay to call you at work."

"Of course, it is," she said warmly. "I saw Tom's ad in the paper. I guess that means you weathered the storm all right?"

"Yes, thank goodness. Only a few loose boards at the marina, and that's really why I called. I know it's awfully late notice, but Tom has a night off tomorrow so we've decided to throw a post-hurricane cookout. We'd love it if you'd join us. Oops—hold on."

While Mary said something about not playing with "that" and two little voices clamored for something Stephanie couldn't quite decipher, something involving "Miss Steppy" and "posh," she considered her plans. The excitement on tap for tomorrow was no different from any of the last twenty-one straight days—work until she couldn't see straight, stop for takeout on the way home, and spend a nice, relaxing evening with her laptop and files. If she didn't start following some of the advice she had given Brett, she would soon be walking her own job-burnout line.

"I'd love to," she answered when she had Mary's attention again. "Is there anything I can bring?"

"Not a thing except, mmm, maybe some nail polish?" Mary asked, sounding half-apologetic. "The girls keep begging to have their nails done again. I did it once, but I'm just a mommy. I don't have the right touch. Or maybe it's the color."

The story drew a laugh from both of them. She would love to paint the girls' nails, she said. "I'll be there at six."

After they hung up, she buzzed her receptionist. "Ralinda, could you pull Paul Mason's address for me? And clear my calendar tomorrow afternoon. I'm knocking off early and won't be in till Monday."

Seconds later, her willowy right-hand woman appeared

in her doorway with the information. "You deserve a week-end off. You've worked, what? Sixteen days straight?"

Anything more might qualify her for martyrdom, so Stephanie kept mum on the real number. She turned instead to her computer where a stiletto-wielding brunette crept across the screen, smacked the corporate dragon on the nose and made off with all his gold. Stephanie smoth-ered a smile and hit the Delete key. Space Tech frowned on personal computer use, but that hadn't stopped the cartoon from flooding company e-mails or slowed the goodwill generated by her hurricane policy. She thought it might have even lessened the sting of the reorganization she'd implemented. As for the caricature's source, John Sanders was the only local with the whole story and she refused to jeopardize the founder's support by asking him about it.

OKAY, SO SHE MIGHT have gone a little overboard, Stepha-nie admitted with a glance at the hamper strapped into the passenger seat of her company car. But baby clothes, gift certificates and assorted goodies were the least she could buy for a man with a hole in the roof of his trailer and a brand-new baby at home. Especially since he had provided the impetus for her first major success at Space Tech.

Trouble was, she couldn't find Paul Mason.

She slowed in front of a neat brick rambler at the address her GPS navigational system and the efficient Ralinda swore was correct. There was nary a trailer in sight. Nor a single damaged and blue-tarped roof. Intend-ing to double-check the address, she edged her car to the curb just in time to realize she had been duped.

Her tummy did a quick tuck and roll as Paul Mason, dressed like something out of *GQ*, emerged from a house that did not have four wheels. Stephanie eyed the woman on his arm and swore she'd eat her imitation Coach purse if the girl had given birth within the last year. With no baby carrier to slow them down, the carefree couple climbed into an SUV so new it bore dealer tags.

Had Paul used money from the hurricane relief fund to buy a new car?

In light of all his other lies, Stephanie was certain of it. She hunkered below the headrest where she fought angry tears. She had personally approved the guard's time off and the money to repair his nonexistent trailer. Her gullibility would undo all she had accomplished, and when Corporate learned of the fiasco, not only would they pull the plug on the relief program, she could kiss her dreams of advancement goodbye.

Or worse.

Worse, how? Her mind immediately produced several scenarios, one of which earned her an all-expense-paid vacation in a federal prison. While that might be a little far-fetched, this was definitely a crisis, one she needed to drop everything to handle.

She drummed the steering wheel and concentrated on breathing.

What next?

She would call Mary Jenkins and beg out of the barbecue.

She would head back to the office.

She would spend the weekend verifying the claims of other so-called hurricane victims and praying Paul was the only cheat.

Her fingers stopped drumming.

She would do nothing of the sort.

Wasn't this exactly what she had warned Brett about?

There was always a crisis at work. Some were bigger than others—and this one was huge—but she could either leave it at work, or surrender her life to it. Sure, she could spend the weekend building a case against Paul Mason and anyone else who was involved but, no matter what, the situation would still be there on Monday.

It was time to follow her own advice.

That didn't make the choice any easier. By the time she reached the little beach house she called home, her shoulders throbbed beneath twin yokes of tension and disappointment. She changed into jogging shorts and shoes. Pounding her stress into the packed sand at the water's edge, she ran until she felt ready to pick up the pieces of her ruined weekend.

BRETT'S EYES NARROWED at the unfamiliar 300-Series sedan parked in front of Tom and Mary's house. His hand was halfway to the radio mike before he remembered he was off duty, not driving his patrol car.

He tried telling himself he had been working too hard, but the excuse made him shift uncomfortably. Truth was, he had worked his share of overtime, but there had been times when he wasn't so exhausted that sleep claimed him almost before he reached his bed. On those nights, he headed for Sticks N Tips where he and his fellow officers killed a few hours, threw a few darts and tipped back a few beers.

It was all Stephanie's fault.

Just thinking of the curvaceous elf with the amazing blue eyes made his heart race. He had kissed enough women to know when the electricity was there, and Stephanie's kiss had thrown all his switches. Likewise, he had given the curvy brunette some of his best stuff and was willing to bet he'd unleashed a current in her the likes of which she'd never known. But how did she respond?

"Don't call me, I'll call you."

Her sharp barb had drawn so much blood he had resorted to the procedures manual. True, there was nothing in the first aid book about *drinking* the alcohol, but it worked very well when applied directly to his wounded pride. His self-esteem had healed with barely a scar. He was ready to forget her, or give her a call.

His finger hesitated over the keypad of his cell phone.

Just in time to let him off the hook, a tummy on two legs, followed by its mirror image with a dad in hot pursuit, roared around the corner of the house. Holstering his cell, he watched Tom scoop the runaway off the ground and toss a twin—Brenda or Barbara, Brett could never keep them straight—into the air, catching her as easily as if he'd been doing it all her life...which he had. Brett swallowed his envy. It was time to join the fray.

"Unca Brett! Unca Brett!"

Scrambling out of their father's arms, the twins were on approach the moment he cleared the front bumper. Divide and conquer was the theme as each slammed into a knee and tugged. Brett pretended to lose his balance, arcing in slow motion down to the ground where the giggling girls pounced on his chest. Usually, this was the point where they demanded the presents Unca Brett always provided. But this day, twenty little fingers waggled dangerously close to his eyes while the twins bounced up and down yelling, "Posh! Posh!"

He didn't have a clue what they were talking about and it must have shown on his face.

Chuckling, Tom said, "Stacie. That girl we met at the storm shelter? She painted their nails a little while ago. It's all they can talk about."

"Polish?" Brett mock-roared to the girls' delighted squeals. "Gimme those hands. I'll eat 'em up." Pretending to munch, monster-style, on little fingers, he noticed that whoever this Stacie was, she had used a different shade of pink with each girl. His monster-grin widened. Finally. He had a clue as to which twin was which.

"I don't think you've mentioned her," he said while he and Tom continued tussling with the twins.

"I might have if you'd come around more often." Tom tried to jab Brett with his elbow.

Brett ducked the blow but not the blame. "My bad," he said. "I'll do better."

"You should. Brenda—" Tom's chin dipped to the darkly polished twin "—and Barbara miss their favorite uncle."

"I miss them, too," he admitted before surrendering to another round of tickles. By the time he and Tom were breathless and the girls worn out, he had heard enough about the virtuous Stacie to raise questions.

"You and Mary aren't setting me up, are you?"

"Nah." Tom gave his head a shake that said more than words. "She's not your type. Mary invited her tonight 'cause she's new in town and she was so nice at the shelter an' all. Plus, the girls like her."

From all accounts, the amazing Stacie had saved his friends from a horrifying night out in the storm, single-handedly organized the chaos of the shelter, and stolen the hearts of his two best girls. Even Seminole loved her, according to Tom, who reported the dog had spent the night at the foot of her sleeping bag. Stacie sounded exactly like the type of woman he needed in his life. Brett shrugged. If he weren't so hung up on a certain brunette, he might even be interested.

As other guests began to arrive, Tom steered the party around to the covered pool and patio where Brett staked out a seat in clear view of the goings-on. Munching on salsa and chips, he made small talk with friends he hadn't seen in far too long while watching over the twins who sat at his feet busily divesting Unca Brett's presents of their clothes. Once the brand-new dolls were suitably naked, the twins toted them to the house. Through tempered glass, Brett caught the flash of a shapely wrist, but nothing more until the door opened some time later to spill out two giggling and cooing girls. They rushed to him, determined he admire the matching "posh" sported by their babies.

He was on his feet, his patented here-let-me-help-you smile plastered in place the next time sliding glass rattled in its tracks. But one glance at an oddly familiar tush backing through the door, followed by arms that held platters of burgers and dogs instead of what he wanted them to, and he spun aside. Shooting a casual wave to no one in particular, he strode purposefully to the other end of the deck where a cedar post offered support. He shuttered his eyes behind dark sunglasses, wishing they could cloak him in invisibility until he figured things out. He hadn't made much headway before the crowd parted enough to let twin-toting Tom and Mary pass into view. Brett glimpsed the graceful ankles and dark hair of someone trailing in their wake. His gut tightened.

"Brett." Tom stepped to one side. "I'd like you to meet Stacie Bryant."

"Stephanie." Brett and Stephanie spoke in the same instant.

"Stephanie? Oh," Tom repeated vacantly. "Sorry about that." He turned to the newcomer. "I'm very bad with names," he explained with a red-faced shrug.

The tops of Mary's eyebrows rose above the rim of her sunglasses while her look bounced between her two guests. "He's right, you know. He's always been bad with names. But…you've met?"

"Before the storm," Brett answered as the dominos in his mind rearranged themselves into a new pattern. He trusted Tom's judgment. And Mary's. His friends thought Stephanie was all-about-the-other-guy. They would laugh if he called her a "me, me" girl. Which meant he had misjudged Stephanie from the moment they met. His throat closed.

He cleared it before he turned to her. "How have you been? Settled into that new job yet?"

"Not quite," she answered. A look he could not decipher crossed her face before the lips he longed to kiss shifted into a guarded smile. "This is the first day I've had off in weeks. How about yourself? Still saving damsels in distress from wicked con men and half-crazed drivers?"

He followed her lead, stumbling through an abbreviated and nearly lighthearted version of the hurricane's aftermath while behind dark glasses, his eyes narrowed. Something was bothering her. He could tell by the way worry tied a knot into the space between her brows. Was it him? Nah, he had backed off, just like she'd asked him to. He hadn't written that frown on her face…though he'd be happy to help erase it.

"There's a story in here somewhere," Tom speculated as both he and his wife looked at him with question marks in their eyes. Brett kept his mouth shut. "But…I have a ton of burgers to burn."

Mary sniffed at Brenda. "And someone has a stinky diaper." She turned to Brett. "Could you introduce Stephanie to the rest of our guests?"

"And get her something to drink," said Tom before host and hostess faded into the rest of the party.

Protestations aside, Brett knew when he was being set up. Apparently, so did Stephanie.

"What are we supposed to do now?" she asked. Though her brow remained knotted, her smile slid to one side suggestively. "Fall all over each other? Disappear arm in arm? Announce we've found our soul mates over dessert?"

He didn't see anything wrong with that plan, but a simple phone call might have accomplished the same thing weeks ago. She hadn't made it.

"Wouldn't that give them a well-deserved shock?" Despite her carefree grin, he couldn't shake the feeling that something was disturbing her. "Are you all right?"

Her shoulders rounded, her smile dimming at the same time. "It's Friday, you know. If anything can go wrong at work, it will always happen on Friday afternoon so you have all weekend to worry over it."

"Any way I can help?" There were a lot of things he wanted to help her with. Work wasn't one of them, but it was a place to start.

She tugged the corner of her bottom lip between even teeth. "Actually, no."

He watched her straighten, run a hand through her hair, and shake her shoulders the way someone might shrug off an unwanted sweater. "Let's just enjoy ourselves tonight."

Something was definitely up, but if she wanted to bury her woes, he was her man. He scrutinized the clusters of longtime friends and friends of friends, dutifully cataloging the position of each unattached competitor and two or three attached males who also required a wide berth. "Let's start by introducing you to the rest of the gang. What do you say?"

Sensing a break in the nearest conversation, he jumped in with both feet. His hands were another matter. He jammed them in his pockets so they wouldn't reach out and touch someone who had made it clear she did not want to be touched. At least, not by him.

"Hey, guys. Have you met Stephanie?" he asked the group.

After making introductions, he concentrated on the way the sun burned his back so he wouldn't have to think about the way even her distracted warmth brought smiles to everyone she met. He left her safely chatting with a clutch of women while he fetched drinks, but the evening breeze had shifted by the time he returned. The fragrance of hibiscus and plumeria drifted elsewhere. The powdery scent of her perfume filled his nose. Hoping for a reprieve, he steered them closer to the pool where he lasted until the setting sun stopped glinting off the water and turned to sparkles in her dark curls.

"Let's get something to eat," he suggested.

They worked their way back to the grill in time to snag chairs next to Mary and the girls. Brett, thankful for something new to keep his hands occupied, lifted a dripping burger halfway to his mouth. Just as he was about to take a bite he realized Stephanie had propped her sunglasses on top of her head. With his first real look at her face, the burger found its way back to the plate uneaten.

After checking the color of nail polish on little fingers, he danced a potato chip onto Barbara's plate and kept the twins amused while Mary and Stephanie chatted across the table. They spoke as if nothing were amiss in the entire world, but he had had the woman of his dreams in handcuffs. Not even arrest or a looming hurricane had dimmed her shining blues, not the way they were clouded now. When Mary announced bedtime for the two sleepy toddlers and Stephanie insisted on helping, he studied the brunette's retreating figure.

Whatever was bothering her, it wasn't life or death. Those were beyond his powers anyway. But work? That was something he could deal with. As a lifelong resident, he knew practically everyone. Between his pals on the force and the rest of his friends, they knew everyone else. If she was having problems in the office, he would call in as many favors as required to fix things. And that would give him time to work on the relationship he was certain they were destined to share, now that he knew she was exactly the type of woman he wanted in his life.

In the meantime, he would take things slow and easy. He had a year to make this work. A year before her next assignment. Satisfied with his plan, he tipped his chair back and waited for Stephanie to emerge from the house.

A smile spread across his face, but Mary was flying solo when the sliding glass opened and she took the seat opposite him.

"I'm sorry, Brett," she said. "She left."

The bite of hamburger he had managed thunked into his stomach like a lead weight. This wasn't part of the plan. Not part of the plan at all. Of course, falling for Stephanie was not in his plan either, especially when she had so obviously *not* fallen for him.

Stars barely twinkled in the darkening sky when he pleaded an early-morning shift and made his excuses.

SEA OATS AND SAND DUNES lined the path, blocking the night breeze and muffling the sound of the breakers. Stephanie swept a tangle of hair from her face and plowed on, determined to dip her toes in the eddying tide. She would not venture into deeper water where who knew what predators prowled the dark currents. But she needed to stand on the beach, hear the waves thunder ashore and feel salt spray on her face.

Maybe the ocean would give her strength. With overwhelming problems on all sides, she would take help where she could find it.

Thanks to Paul Mason, her career shifted like the sand beneath her feet. As bad as that was, all thought of felonious guards had ceased the moment she spied Brett at Tom and Mary's. One look through the front window at the tall, muscular cop lying on the ground bouncing the twins on his wide chest had added a whole new dimension to her woes. The man who personified "macho" could be tender with little kids. Who would have guessed? The insight toppled her reservations about him. It had taken every ounce of her dwindling resolve not to throw herself into Brett's arms and demand that he whisk her away and kiss her until lightning bolts flashed from the sky, or at least give her a call.

Wasn't this a fine mess?

She stepped onto the wooden observation deck at the end of the last dune. The horizon and the ocean barely sighed beneath the moonless sky. Disappointment drove her to lean heavily against the railing.

Where was the power? Where was the raw fury she had witnessed from this very deck in the days following the hurricane? If she couldn't draw strength from the ocean, how would she face her situation?

She had the training, she reminded herself. She had the experience and fortitude to deal with the likes of a miscreant guard. Trouble was, by exposing his fraud, she would also be risking her own career…and that meant risking the time she needed to build a relationship with a certain cop.

Turning in Paul Mason was the right thing to do. She knew it.

But could she do it?

"Stephanie."

The waves whispered her name. The ocean was on her side after all. She straightened, drew in a deep breath of salty air and felt a reserve of her own strength unfurl.

Paul Mason was toast!

"Stephanie."

Okay, so that wasn't the ocean talking. She was still strong. She was still capable. She was still…a woman standing alone on the beach in the middle of the night.

She spun to see a tall shadow emerge from the pathway through the dunes. Before her eyes had time to register the image and send it to her brain for decoding, her heart recognized the broad-shouldered silhouette. Her fears hushed.

"Brett." Problem number two in all his glory. "You nearly scared me to death," she said as soon as she could breathe. "What are you doing here?"

"I didn't mean to frighten you. I can leave if you want."

"No. No, that's okay." He hadn't answered her question. "Brett, what are you doing here?" Had the man who would not call actually followed her?

"There's usually good surf just south of here."

What she knew about surfing wouldn't fill a thimble, but he wasn't carrying a board and she was pretty sure the sport required one. She gave the ocean a second glance. "Looks a little flat tonight."

He moved to her side. "The surf is decidedly not up."

"So, why are you here?" she asked, hopeful.

"I have a few things on my mind." His voice dropped. "You put most of them there."

"Me?" She held her breath.

"I've been giving some thought to the things you said about job burnout."

"Oh." If they were going to waste a perfectly good night on the beach talking about work, she would never give advice again.

"Haven't done much about it, but I am thinking about it."

"O-kay."

"Plus, you looked so worried at the cookout. You said it was your job, but I wanted to help if I can."

"Oh. That." And here she was, thinking maybe he wanted to kiss her. Her exhale sounded as ragged as she felt.

Work. They would talk about work.

"Because of the hurricane, I convinced the home office to extend emergency aid—time off and other things. They were against it, but—"

"—you swept them off their feet."

She smiled. Sweeping Brett off his feet wasn't nearly so easy. "I appealed to their wallets. In the long run, we give a little and save a lot."

"Sounds like smart business, but I guess something went wrong?"

"The usual. Someone—the security guard who showed me around my first day, actually—took advantage. I found out after work and, well, it threw me."

"You going to press charges? If you need help arresting the guy—"

"Whoa, cowboy!" She let her hand settle on his arm. For a minute there, she'd forgotten she was talking to a cop. Of course, he would see everything in black and white, but this problem had several facets. "I was more concerned about Corporate pulling the plug on the assistance program. And, to be frank, how it would affect me."

"You?" He paused. "Oh, yeah. Your promotion."

His voice carried a hard edge that made her retrieve her

hand. "I've worked hard to get where I am," she said crossly. "But I could get fired for this. Corporate could order me back to Ohio. Either way, I'd lose all that I've worked for."

"But you have to turn him in. You're not the kind of girl to—"

"I'm not sure you know what kind of girl I am, Brett." She felt, rather than saw, him bristle. "But, yeah, I'm going to do it. I have to investigate a little further, make sure no one else has abused the program."

"Or that he hasn't done anything worse."

The idea elicited an inward groan. "Why didn't I think of that?"

Her rhetorical question drew an answer from Brett. "Because you're not a cop. If you give me his name, I'll check him out for you. See if anything obvious pops up."

"Can't." She shook her head. "Not until I inform management."

"Well, at least see what kind of house he owns." He leaned back from the railing. "Check out the car he drives. You probably know his salary. Can he afford his lifestyle?"

"Probably not," she whispered, remembering the affordable trailer Paul claimed to live in, the reality of his upscale neighborhood, the brand-new SUV.

Brett turned to face her. "It's that serious? They'd really transfer you?"

She didn't want to think about it, but she needed to be honest. "The last HR manager left in a hurry. Very hush-hush. Rumor says he was let go. A transfer is the *best* I could hope for."

"That kind of changes things," he said quietly.

It was exactly what she was afraid of.

She stilled when his body shifted close enough that she felt his breath stir gentle currents through her hair. His arms slipped around her waist and drew her to him. The night was so black she could not read his eyes, but she sensed a goodbye kiss in the offing. If so, she'd make it a good one.

She tipped her head to his and felt his lips brush hers. His mouth pressed against her own, so firm, so strong that her lips parted willingly when he teased them. He tasted of mint and spice and salt, and she sighed into a kiss that was sweet and light.

Hesitantly, she explored his mouth. Because this was a goodbye kiss, because she'd never have the opportunity again, she trailed her fingertips over the sandpaper of his cheek and traced the outline of his jaw. At her touch, he whispered her name.

Sweet and light gave way to urgent and demanding.

One of his hands cupped her face, the other slipped through her hair to guide her even closer. His touch was enough to drive her mad with longing, and her breasts swelled at the low rumble that rose from his chest. Their tongues danced them to the edge of a world where kissing wasn't enough.

"Brett, I—"

"Right. You're right." His hands settled onto her shoulders until he held her at arm's length.

In this case, being right wasn't as much fun as it usually was. She sought his chest where she nestled in the crook of his arm, listening to the beat of their hearts while they watched stars blink in the night sky.

"How about dinner when I get off work tomorrow?" he asked after a few minutes.

Dinner sounded like a beginning, not an end.

"Sounds good," she agreed.

Chapter Eight

Dreams of a certain hunky cop vied with nightmares about wayward guards until Stephanie woke craving chocolate Saturday morning. Hours later her fingers fumbled with the buttons of a chocolate-brown pencil skirt, but she told herself it was uncertainty, not her date, that made her heart race and her mouth water for something sweet.

"Seven o'clock," Brett had said.

"Dinner," he had said.

Why hadn't she asked where they were headed? Tracing the outline of her lips with one finger, she stumbled over the truth. She hadn't asked because she had been a little distracted at the time. All that kissing had numbed her brain right along with her mouth. "Questions first, then kisses" would be her new motto.

A few minutes before seven, she gave her head a rueful shake at the shiny black Avalanche that pulled to the curb in front of her house. The long swath of fabric narrowly encasing her lower half was no match for a tall SUV. She couldn't climb aboard without making a fool of herself, and that was one trick she wanted to avoid. So, no matter where they were headed, a change of clothes was on the menu.

Brett's feet struck the ground on the far side of the vehicle. She watched until he stepped around the back bumper and into full view. Thoughts of her own attire faded as her mouth went dry and her body stilled.

She was willing to bet her date looked better in Banana Republic and J. Crew than Michelangelo's *David* ever could. What better clothes to showcase slim hips and muscular thighs? What could possibly display broad shoulders to better advantage? She let her eyes roam from Brett's sculpted and freshly shaved jaw to his dark, wavy hair. Her palms itched to press themselves against his chest.

Stephanie shook her head and reminded herself to breathe. The doorbell rang.

"I'm coming," she called out, and sped to answer the bell.

"Hey." Brett loomed in her open doorway. "Am I too early?"

One hand fluttered as she imagined the finely honed muscles that must lay beneath the well-pressed fabric of his shirt. She trapped the protesting fingers and led them to safety behind her back. "You're right on time, but I need a few minutes to change."

"Why?" He tugged off sunglasses as he stepped into her living room.

"Your truck. It's so…" She followed his jawline until she reached his devastating eyes. The appreciative look she found there sent her tongue on a quick trip around her lips.

"Big," she managed just as a chill swept through her. She ran a smoothing hand over her skirt while she summoned up the ability to speak. "Your truck is so, uh, tall that I'd have to make like a mountain goat to get into it wearing this."

"Not a problem," Brett said with a shrug. "I'll wait if

you want. But you should know, I think what you're wearing looks great."

Stephanie weighed the odds of making a fool of herself versus choosing something that might not bring that particular gleam back into his eyes. She could handle foolishness, she decided.

She needn't have worried. As she stood at the door of his truck pondering the best way to hike her skirt and scramble into the cab while retaining some measure of decorum, Brett swept her into his arms and deposited her in the passenger seat. He did so without even breathing hard. Which was fine with Stephanie—his touch made her breathe hard enough for the both of them.

They sped over the causeway, turning south onto a black ribbon of Tarmac that trailed the river's edge. "Old U.S. One," Brett called it as they wove slowly beneath and between ancient oak trees on a road never intended for wide-bodied SUV's. Few of the original shotgun-style houses remained, he said, pointing to one where a front porch crumpled beneath a tangle of kudzu. A battalion of heavy equipment was parked nearby. As riverfront values soared, he explained, so did the minimansions built by local politicians and businessmen to replace the teardowns.

"That one belongs to John Sanders." He slowed the Avalanche to a crawl.

A wide veranda and functional, slatted shutters dated the home to a pre-air-conditioning era but the wood-frame house had aged gently beneath its canopy of immense trees.

"I've met him," she offered, picturing ramrod-straight shoulders and a garrulous smile. "We've spoken several times in the last few weeks."

"I thought he retired ages ago." Brett gave the SUV a

bit more gas as they hit a straighter stretch. "Doesn't surprise me that he'd keep a hand in, though. Built that company into what it is today. It's the county's biggest employer." He caught himself with a half laugh that made her grin. "But I guess you know that already."

"Yeah," she said. "I think I heard that somewhere." Beneath her seat belt, she shifted. Thinking of John Sanders reminded her of work and its problems. Problems she could have spent the weekend investigating, but had put on hold to be with Brett. She refused to let her troubles interfere with the evening and deliberately twisted until she could look at her date without turning her head.

She loved everything about Brett's face, from the tumble of dark hair over his eyes to the rugged edge of his chin. She had never felt so protected as she did with his strong arms wrapped around her, her face pressed against his broad, solid chest. The memory of their embrace rushed back and she recalled the way his long legs pressed against hers. She ached to feel that way again.

One tire thunked into a pothole and bounced out, jarring some sense into her. He wasn't taking her to his place for "pasta and whatever." And she couldn't seduce him in a public restaurant. Not unless it was called The Horny Toad.

"So where are we going?" she asked hopefully.

"There's a little place I like on the river down south. I haven't been there in a while and thought we'd check it out. It's called The Yellow Dog Café," he said.

The name was close enough to make one of her eyebrows dip just as Brett glanced her way.

"It's a nice place. Trust me." He pointed to the river where a pair of hooked dorsal fins sliced through the water.

"Dolphin," he said as they disappeared. "They'll surface again in a minute."

She settled further into the bucket seat and pretended to watch the large mammals cavort in the river. If Brett said The Yellow Dog was okay, it was fine with her. She would trust him with dinner. But, she wondered, as he treated her to a minitravelogue based on a bottomless well of knowledge about the area, could she trust him with her heart?

Maybe. Maybe not.

The host at the restaurant probably thought he was being Mr. Excellent Maître d' when he greeted Brett by name. Surely the man had no clue he was waving red flags as he led them to a coveted corner table overlooking white sails and blue water.

Stephanie glanced across the linen tablecloth and sparkling silver to the handsome man who ordered wine and appetizers without so much as cracking open his copy of the leather-bound menu. He had been to the restaurant often enough that the staff knew him by name. And how many of those times had he been alone?

"So, Brett." In the glow of his warm smile, her courage plummeted. She gulped water from a crystal goblet. "What is this, your standard first-date place?" It hurt that she didn't mean more to him.

His head tilted just enough to throw her heart off balance. "What?" he asked.

"You've been here before," she said. It took a surprising effort to keep the crush of disappointment from her voice. "The host knows you."

Brett nodded to another table where the dark-haired man was distributing menus to newcomers. "We've been on a first-name basis ever since I busted him for peddling drugs at the junior high school."

She bolted straight up in her chair. "Really?" Her head yo-yoed back and forth between the man and a smiling Brett. "You're teasing."

"You deserved it," he said. "I take first dates to a movie—no talking required. If that goes well, we see each other a couple of times before I introduce her to my friends." He reached across the table to take her hands in his. "I think we're past all that, don't you?"

His voice warmed her to the core and set off a series of tremors that shook the foundations of her structured future. "Yes," she whispered. "We definitely are."

"But to answer your question, I did bring a date here once. She didn't like it so we didn't come back. Mostly I used to come here with my folks before they moved to the Carolinas. It was kind of their place, if you know what I mean. Do you like it?"

Fresh flowers sprang from wall sconces, hundreds of framed dog photos lined the stair rails, and kitschy marionettes danced from overhead beams. Everything about the restaurant, from the polished oak bar to the stairs that led to an outside deck, promised solidity and permanence. The eclectic collections only added to the allure, as did immense windows offering spectacular views of a river as changeable as the man seated across the table.

"What's not to like?" she asked.

When their waiter slipped bowls of fragrant chowder before them, Stephanie's eyes fell to the pale gold crackers adorning the crockery. Dog-shaped, they were poised on the rims as if ready to leap. Thinking the crackers could be either one of them, she smiled up at Brett who quirked his eyebrows in acknowledgment.

One taste of the pink soup, though—rich and thick with crab—and her smile faded.

"Oh, this is wonderful," she murmured between spoonfuls. "What idiot dissed your favorite restaurant?"

For the first time since they'd met, her self-assured date looked a little out of his element. "You might know her," he said.

Despite the warning, she prompted him. "Yes?"

"Deb Peters."

"My real estate agent? The woman who swore I'd never have to worry about hurricanes? Who conveniently forgot to mention the storm that nearly destroyed the house she sold to Space Tech? That Deb Peters?" Her simmering distrust of the woman she once considered a potential friend morphed into full-fledged, green-tinged dislike. Stephanie grasped her wineglass, forcing herself to sip slowly when she really wanted to chug it all and ask for more.

Maybe she shouldn't ask about first dates. Maybe she should ask about last ones.

"How long has it been since you and Debbie, you know, quit seeing each other?" She held her breath while, across the table, Brett blew out his.

"A year. Maybe more."

She exhaled. A year was certainly long enough to get over someone so unappreciative though Stephanie felt certain she'd *never* forgive the woman. She knew better than to ask, but her mind latched on to the image of Brett with the tall blonde and it wouldn't let go. There had to be others. "And since then?" she asked.

"No one," he said firmly. His blue eyes held hers while the waiter whisked empty bowls from the table, replacing them with chilled salad plates.

"And you?" he asked. "Any ex-boyfriends going to descend from Ohio to steal you away?"

"Remember me? I lived with my parents." The quip

earned a laugh, but Brett kept looking at her, waiting for a real answer. She studied her plate where lemony vinaigrette slicked greens and red beans. The pages in her love diary were embarrassingly empty. She sighed.

"It's been all work and no play for far too long," she admitted slowly. "I hired on at Space Tech right out of college. Between work and getting my master's, and work and writing my thesis, and work…" She shrugged. "I haven't had much time for anything else."

She frowned as a familiar tightness settled onto her shoulders. Talking about her job would ruin the whole evening if she let it, and a single glance at Brett told her what a terrible mistake that would be. Deliberately, she straightened to issue a challenge.

"Pick a topic. Anything but work. Even religion and politics are fair game. Go."

After a pause long enough to let her know they were both thinking the same thing, amusement danced in Brett's eyes. "Fly fishing," he said with a grin that could disarm a bandit.

Not what she would have chosen, but she'd laid down the rules. Now she had to follow them. "I've always wondered, how is that different from regular fishing?"

A waggish, horrified look dropped over his features. "You've never been fishing? Ever?" When she shook her head, he continued. "Everyone who lives in Florida has to fish. It's a state law. As a police officer, it's my job to uphold the law so, unless you want me to arrest you—"

"Again?" She clutched at her heart and aimed a finger. "No shop talk, remember."

"—I'll have to introduce you to the sport. How about tomorrow?"

With another whole day to kill before Monday, floating down the river in a boat seemed like an excellent idea.

"Sounds good to me," she agreed.

"Great." Brett grinned. "I'll pick you up at seven."

"In the morning? That's awfully early for the weekend," she protested.

"It's all part of the game." Brett leaned back in his chair, his lips straightening as he assessed her willingness to go along with the plan.

The urge to restore his trademark smile moved Stephanie to push aside any misgivings about the hour. "Okay," she said, brightening when he grinned.

"I'll bring the boots," he added.

Before she could ask why, their entrées appeared and, for the next few minutes, they were busy savoring the results of a talented chef. Between bites, they spoke of families and school and hobbies, but the conversation never did circle back to fishing before dinner was over and it was time to go. By then, Stephanie was trying to gather enough courage to ask Brett back to her place.

FROM A REASONABLE two steps behind, Brett watched Stephanie pick her way across the crushed-shell parking lot without complaining—not even once—about her shoes.

Deb had. Boy, had she ever!

He frowned at the memory. All through a dinner she'd barely touched, the rail-thin blonde had ranted about a nearly invisible scratch on one of her high heels. If he had to point to the moment that marked the beginning of the end for them, it was dinner at The Yellow Dog. Yet here he was, starting a new relationship right where the other one had crashed and burned. The thought slowed his steps.

Is that what he wanted with Stephanie, a relationship? He picked up a palm-size oyster shell and skipped it across the parking lot. This might be their first official date, but he knew they had potential. While she was independent to a fault, insisting she could handle things that he could easily take care of for her, he had to admire her spunk. She was also smart and witty, and they made each other laugh. What more could a man ask for?

A stir below his belt reminded him of exactly what else he wanted. He shrugged. Once they got to know each other better, sex with Stephanie would be as inevitable as an incoming tide. Still, he didn't want to rush things, even if he ached to hold her.

He saw a chance to do just that and seized it as he reached past her to open the truck door. When he lifted her into his arms, her powdery floral scent filled his head until he pretended to stagger so he could hold on to her a little longer. A body like hers deserved a reward, he decided. He gave her the only one he had and stole a teasing kiss before settling her on the leather seat.

At least, he intended to steal a kiss and back off. Keeping his distance was not as easy as he'd thought it would be. He kissed her until they were both in danger of getting in over their heads right there in the parking lot. Breathless, they pulled back, and he let his eyes roam the length of her. From curls his hands wanted to lose themselves in, to sensuous curves that made every part of him ache, to the most elegant ankles he'd ever seen, she was everything he had ever wanted all rolled into one small package. Loving this girl would be easy.

Brett stepped back and closed the truck's door. The L-word was definitely off limits for a first date, but Stephanie was different from anyone he had ever known before. So different, in fact, that he could hardly wait to introduce her to the people who watched his back. He knew the guys would be glad for him. Jake and his pals had sniffed out

Deb's self-centeredness from their first encounter and pounced on her like a pack of hungry wolves. And when that relationship had failed, they'd predicted he was doomed to date the same type of woman over and over and over. They would see how wrong they had been once they met Stephanie.

Sliding behind the wheel he asked, "How about a drink before we call it a night?"

A broad smile broke across his face when his buds at Sticks N Tips got their first look at Stephanie. She was quite an eyeful. The thought straightened his spine and filled his chest.

Since she seemed a bit overwhelmed when several of the guys muscled their way through the crowded bar to pay their respects, he draped his arm possessively about her shoulders and pulled her close enough that there would be no doubt. She was his and he was not about to share, not even with his pals on the force—especially not with his pals on the force.

"Beer?" he asked. Without waiting for an answer, he flashed the gal behind the bar two fingers before steering Stephanie toward the corner where his usual spot was empty and waiting at Jake's table.

"Stephanie Bryant, I'd like you to meet Jake Davis, our training officer. Jake, this is Stephanie Bryant. She moved into the Henson place."

Jake disentangled enough of himself from Becca, his latest good-time girl, to half rise. He stretched a hand across a table littered with beer mugs and shot glasses. "Ma'am," he said.

Brett held Stephanie close enough to feel her stiffen. He grinned, remembering her reaction the day they'd met. He couldn't fault the reserved, "Pleasure," she offered Jake in return, but wished he could remind her that his mentor was a senior officer. Despite some rough edges, the man deserved her respect.

As they took their seats, Jake handled the rest of the introductions, leaving Stephanie and the others to trade smiles and polite nods. The second their drinks arrived, Brett slid one of the two frosty mugs over to his date while, across the table, Jake raised his glass in salute.

"Cheers," offered the older cop. After a deep swallow, he asked, "So, Steph-ee, where're you from?"

Brett bit back a smile. Jake found it impossible to forget he was a cop and had just commenced Interrogation 101. A pro, the man would ferret out more information in an hour than Brett could get in a string of dates.

"It's Stephanie, and I'm from Ohio."

Or maybe not.

Brett traded an uneasy glance with Jake, whose presence was so intimidating that people rarely corrected him. Every man on the force knew Stephanie would have to earn the senior officer's approval, and his misuse of her name was part of the process all the wives and girlfriends went through. The ones who lasted endured without complaint. Brett leaned in to whisper caution in his date's ear, but Jake motioned him back.

"Ohio, huh? Waaal…" he drawled, "you're a long way from home, Ste-fanny. What brings you down here?"

If he could, Brett would have told her to ignore the jibe, but one look at his mentor told him to stay out of the fray. Stephanie was on her own as she answered crisply, "A job transfer. I work for Space Tech."

"Oh?" Jake's heavy eyebrows wagged suggestively. "They couldn't find a local girl willing to sit on the boss's lap and take dictation?"

Beside him, Stephanie straightened until she sat primly on her cute fanny. "I *am* the boss, and *you* don't need to be rude."

Brett couldn't stop himself. He lifted his mug to stare a warning over its top and set the ground rules for his date.

"Stephanie is the new head of the HR department. She's from up north so it might be a while before she realizes we don't take ourselves so seriously down here." Jake's nod of approval felt almost as good as the cold liquid that slid down Brett's throat.

"Waaal, I think that calls for another round. Ma treat," Jake insisted.

"Hey, Lincoln!" A voice rose above the general din. "C'mon, man. We need you back here."

Brett twisted in his seat. At the back of the bar, a dart game was forming up. "Some other time," he said, almost shouting to make himself heard.

From across the table came Jake's voice of command. "Go ahead and play a game. Me and Steph-an-ie, here, will get better acquainted."

Brett wasn't certain which one of them he was feeding to the wolves but his response to Jake was so ingrained he was halfway out of his chair before he thought to ask permission of his date. "That okay with you, honey?"

Stephanie sipped her drink before she answered. "Sure. Honey."

The clipped tone told him a kiss was out of the question, not that he would have offered one in front of his pals. He was content with trailing his fingers across shoulders that flinched beneath his touch. "I won't be long," he offered.

No use. Sharp teeth filled the smile she tossed in his direction.

Nursing a Coke—no way was he going back for the

beer he'd left on the table—Brett joined the group in the back room, where the dart game was already underway. Trading good-natured digs with the players, he tried to monitor things at Jake's table without much luck. One or another of his cop buddies always seemed to block his view. The game was tied up when Brett caught a glimpse of dark brown in his peripheral vision. He knocked back a last slug of soda and turned to face Stephanie.

"Ready?" he asked as if the arms folded securely across her chest weren't clue enough.

She didn't speak, merely nodded and spun into reverse.

As they passed Jake's table, Brett eyed his pal who gave him an innocent look that was anything but.

"You okay?" he asked Stephanie once they were outside.

"Fine. I love it when my date abandons me to a game of twenty questions."

Sarcasm was never a good sign. "What happened while I was in the back?" he asked.

"Oh, Jake was exactly what I thought he'd be—rude, insulting. Nice to be left in such good hands. Thanks for that. And you say he's the *finest* officer on the force?"

He hadn't heard Jake's side of the story, but Stephanie's opinion was easy enough to read. He watched as his date practically marched all the way to the truck where she scrambled into the cab before he could cup her elbow, much less anything else. Her hand shot for the radio dial where she spun the volume high enough to block out all conversation during a short ride that was so chilly it required no air-conditioning. The truck barely rolled to a stop before, with a quick, "Thanks for a nice time," she was out of it and halfway up her sidewalk. Brett watched her hips rocket from side to side until she stepped onto her front porch.

Now what? He resisted the urge to scratch his head.

He could follow her. Ask her to talk. Fix things. He eyed the closed door at the end of the walkway. The porch light blinked out. It might be cowardly, but he knew better than to knock on that door tonight.

That left Sticks N Tips. He could drive back to the bar. See what the guys really thought of his woman. Maybe talk to Jake. Or not. If Stephanie had failed the senior officer's interrogation, Brett's gut told him he didn't want to know. Relationship or no, choosing between his gal and his pals was a choice he was not prepared to make.

Dissatisfied with both options, Brett put the truck in gear and headed home.

SLEEP WAS IMPOSSIBLE when you were furious, Stephanie discovered after tossing and turning for hours that seemed to stretch as endlessly as the ocean. She punched her pillow until she felt sorry for it. The tangled mess she'd made of her sheets rivaled anything she and Brett could have done to them. "Would have done to them," she said with a sigh when she finally calmed down long enough to admit she had acted like a jerk.

She hadn't been the only one. The bar had been full of them.

Jake was hardly a class act, but she could avoid him. Brett was the one she was worried about. Though his bad behavior hardly excused her own, she owed him an apology. She spent what was left of the night crafting one that would tell the man who was dangerously close to stealing her heart she was sorry without letting him off the hook for going all testosterone on her the moment he pulled into the parking lot of Sticks N Tips.

At five, she gave up on sleep, ran a hand through her

tousled hair and stretched. Hitting the button on the alarm before it rang, she sat on the edge of her bed. Sunrise was still an hour away but the pitch-black of night had already faded to shades of gray outside her bedroom window.

Would she see him today? Or had their plans collapsed along with their date last night? Either way, the sleepless night lay behind her.

An hour later, she sat at her kitchen table, a cup of coffee growing cold at her fingertips. The morning paper was open to page three, but when the air conditioner riffled the pages, she realized she had been staring at the same article for fifteen minutes without reading a word.

Loud chimes broke her concentration.

She managed to stand without knocking her coffee cup to the floor, but that didn't keep her knees from knocking. He was early. No doubt about that. Had his night been as sleepless as hers? She could only hope.

She glanced down at the T-shirt and shorts she wore over her bathing suit. Good thing for him, she was ready.

Okay, so her speech wasn't quite finished.

Actually, it was two speeches in one. An apology. And a what-for. All the way through the kitchen and living room, she practiced the back half.

"I'm sorry," she said as she pulled the door wide.

"I'm sorry," he echoed as he pulled her into his arms.

Well, I'm glad that's over, she thought in the split-second before his lips claimed hers. His cheeks were unshaven. He tasted like coffee and breath mints. She loved the smell of him and when he stopped kissing her long enough to breathe she leaned into him and inhaled a good whiff of—

Whatever it was, she hated it. With a muffled cough, she pulled away. "*What* are you wearing?" she asked.

She could have written a novel in the blank look he turned on her.

"Shirt. Shorts. Zoris?" he asked, lifting one foot to display a dangling flip-flop.

"Yeah," she said slowly. "Now, don't get offended, but that new cologne? Let's just say, it's not a favorite."

Comprehension animated Brett's face. "It's my special concoction of sunblock and bug spray. You'll need it, too."

Despite her protests, he insisted. "It's the middle of summer. In Florida. We have bugs. The sun burns. Spray the repellant on your clothes, not on your skin." Next, he handed her a bottle marked SPF 45. "I want us to have long lives. So you have to follow the rules. Don't smoke. Wear your seat belt. And put on sun block when you'll be outside. Sunburns are the pits. Plus, they give you cancer."

Okay, so it wasn't mushy-mushy, but it did prove he cared. She especially liked that "us" part. She applied the gooey liquid to her arms and legs, pleasantly surprised when the smell faded as it dried into an invisible barrier.

He doused her hat with bug spray and they were off.

Stephanie wrinkled her nose at the pungent smell that permeated the air as they neared the river. She tried breathing through her mouth, but the taste of rotting grass tossed ashore by Hurricane Arlene was worse than the smell.

It was so not a good day for her nose. Or her feet.

"And we're still wading?" she asked after Brett explained why boots were a necessity. Stingrays inhabited the clear, shallow water. They blended perfectly against sand the color of manila folders.

"Don't step on them," he warned. The creatures often showed their appreciation by impaling careless walkers with their barbed tails.

Stephanie wavered for all of two seconds before she reached a decision. She would follow Brett anywhere.

Anywhere except Sticks N Tips. She had seen enough of the macho jerk he became the moment he set foot in the place. As for Jake, no way would she tolerate the disrespect he had shown or the—

She stopped herself when Brett splashed into the water.

The day was not about Sticks N Tips or Jake.

The day was all about them, and one look at Brett was enough to convince her that she was making the right choice. Beneath a broad-brimmed hat, his eyes shone with happiness. Fishing—wading, she corrected—was important to him. And if he loved it so much, the least she could do was give it a try. Mimicking the slow shuffle step that Brett swore encouraged rays and crabs to get out of their way, she braved the water right behind him.

And it wasn't bad.

Warm water lapped gently at her thighs. A breeze cooled her skin and confined the smell of rotting grass to the shoreline they quickly left behind. In the early morning hush, quiet ruled. An occasional pelican splashed down, soaring almost immediately skyward with a fish dripping from its huge beak. Brett pointed to a spot where seagulls wheeled and dove.

"Fish," he whispered and they ambled in that direction while he demonstrated the basics of fly fishing. Line whipped through the air as he made several casts. He explained what to do in steps that sounded simple, but she was so entranced by tiny shrimp floating in the water that she didn't watch carefully. When he placed the rod in her hands, line went everywhere.

"Here, let me show you." Brett smiled warmly. He slipped in behind her.

The sea life lost its fascination the instant his hard muscles pressed against her back. Fishing became quite a bit more interesting with his strong arms guiding hers. The fly rod did what it needed to do and line sailed where it needed to go with his long fingers firmly covering her own.

"Good job," he murmured. He was showing her how to retrieve the line when something tugged on the other end with enough force to jerk the rod out of her hands. She would have lost it entirely if Brett hadn't been holding it, as well.

"Fish on!" he cheered.

"Yippee!" she yelled. Exhilaration filled her and her heart leaped in her throat as Brett taught her what the sport was all about. Together, they fought the fish until it tired enough to come close. Brett snagged and lifted it, dripping and silver, from the water while Stephanie was still shouting.

"A trout," he pronounced. "A gator trout," he added with a broad grin. "Big enough for a trophy." He placed the slippery fish in her arms while he retrieved the fly from its mouth. "What do you think? Your first fish. It's a beauty!"

Gray and speckled, the trout thrashed weakly and she felt tears begin to well.

"What do we do now?" she asked. "Do we…eat it?"

"Most people would. But this is the granddaddy of all trout. He's made lots of babies and he'll make many more if we let him go. What do you think?"

Stephanie thought she was in love.

Since that was an admission she was not prepared to make, she merely nodded as together they lowered the heaving fish into the water. With their hands on its tail, they gently scooted it back and forth until, as Brett said, "he told them he was ready." Letting go, they watched the monster trout streak through the water and disappear.

"You're awfully good at this," she said some time later. By unspoken agreement, they shuffle-walked toward the shore hand in hand.

"It's a lot of fun, isn't it?"

"Terrific," she answered honestly. "I could do this every day."

"I used to." Brett squinted into the distance. "Tom and I did a lot of fishing when we were growing up. But I haven't been out here in months."

"Oh?" she asked. She waved a hand from turquoise sky to crystal water. "What keeps you from it?"

Brett's face turned teasingly devilish. "You. I seem to be spending all my free time with you these days."

That wasn't true but, suspecting a kiss hung in the balance, she kept her thoughts to herself. He spent most of his off-duty hours at Sticks N Tips. She was certain of that. If he cut the bar scene out of his life, there would be plenty of time for more important things. Things like seeing her. And fishing.

And kissing, she added a few seconds later when Brett pulled her into his arms.

He was mighty good at that, too.

FURIOUS OR IN LOVE—either way, sleep was impossible, Stephanie discovered as she turned her sheets into a twisted mess for the second night straight. She spent most of her sleepless hours mentally playing a game of poker. Instead of aces and jokers, she dealt the pros and cons of falling in love. A husband and family did not figure into her immediate future, but Brett's kisses turned her brain to mush. He was an arrogant, disillusioned cop and, except for Tom and Mary, he had some of the worst friends known to mankind. He was also kind, sweet, funny, good with kids and fish, and she wanted him. She played that against her obligation to Space Tech and lost every hand. There was only one way to win—she had to go all in and hope the world was bluffing when it said you couldn't have it all.

Chapter Nine

After a week of shift work that failed to mesh with Stephanie's dawn-to-midnight schedule, Brett was more convinced than ever that he couldn't have it all. But what was life if not compromise? In his job he did it every day. He clocked a speeder at 80 but issued the ticket for 65 because of a—previously—clean driving record. He let a shoplifter walk away when she gave up the goods. He drove a drunk home before the man got behind the wheel. His relationship with Stephanie was no different. Which explained why, on a Sunday afternoon, he dodged teens on Rollerblades and little old ladies in orthopedic shoes at a craft fair when he really wanted to spend the day in bed with the woman who revved his engine.

Brett tucked Stephanie's latest purchase under his arm and, careful to keep his focus above her shoulders or risk embarrassing himself, followed her mop of curly hair into the next booth.

"Ooh. Homemade soap," she purred. She lifted a bar and sniffed. "Yum."

The image of Stephanie lathered in soap bubbles so engrossed Brett he nearly plowed her over when she came to an abrupt stop.

"Isn't that Mary and the girls? Looks like trouble."

That was putting it mildly. On the opposite side of the street, a small crowd had gathered around a bench where Mary sat with one leg outstretched, a bag of ice pressed to her ankle. A pair of old ladies cooed at the twins, which partially explained their tears.

"Mary!" Stephanie called.

Brett hustled as his date cut a swath through the crowded street.

Mary looked up with a grimace. "Twisted my stupid ankle," she managed through clenched teeth. "Tom went for the car, but I don't know how he'll get it here."

All the treelined streets of Cocoa Village had been barricaded for the area's largest craft fair. White display tents stood wall-to-wall along the sidewalks. Eager shoppers ducked in and out of booths and thronged the town's unique stores.

"I'll take care of that," Brett offered. He whipped out his badge. "Where were you parked?" When Mary pointed, he set off to clear a path. He was signaling people out of the way and Tom's van to the curb by the time he realized he'd left Stephanie alone to deal with two wailing toddlers and an injured woman. He hoped she didn't hate him for it and shot a worried look her way.

One glimpse of the twins happily slurping from juice boxes and waving flags from a nearby craft stand, and Brett breathed relief. The girls were so intent on babbling about Mary's *anka-boo-boo,* they didn't even ask him for a present. But once Tom had helped his wife into the van and started moving Brenda from stroller to car seat, loud protests rent the air.

"No, Daddy! Cowns. You proms."

"They mean you promised to let them see the clowns,"

Stephanie interpreted while Brett tried not to gawk. "Why not let us do that while you take Mary to the hospital and get that foot X-rayed."

There really was no other choice.

As their official "Unca," Brett expected to handle the bulk of the twins' care, but Stephanie took the job to heart.

"I think I saw a place where we can get our faces painted and see some ponies," she enthused. "What do you say, Brenda? Barbara? Should we go?"

"Go, Miss Steppy. Pons, Miss Steppy." The twins were all for it.

Brett tagged along as Stephanie led the way to an area of the craft fair he had never visited. Beneath shade trees that had stood far longer than Cocoa had been a village, they indulged the girls with wands and tiaras from the fairy booth. The girls giggled happily while they rode ponies, shared towering cones of cotton candy, had their faces painted by a clown wearing fire-engine-red hair and a goofy grin.

Brett was so impressed by Stephanie's softer side he thought another outing might be fun. They were helping the girls dangle magnets into a wading pool to fish for prizes when he suggested taking the twins on a *real* fishing trip. The look Stephanie shot him reminded him of an expression he had seen on his mom's face more than once, but he didn't have time to decipher it because Barbara decided two minutes of "fishing" was enough, dropped her plastic rod and trotted for the ponies while Brenda opted for the clowns. Brett corralled one twin, Stephanie the other, and they spent the rest of the day riding kiddie rides, feasting on hot dogs and choosing T-shirts embroidered with the girls' names.

By the time Tom called to say Mary's ankle was only

sprained and her mom was on her way to help out, the twins dozed in their stroller, the crafters were disassembling their booths, and Brett knew he was in love. The thought scared the bejesus out of him.

Ever since the hurricane—before, if he were honest—he'd been thinking in terms of home and family. He wanted the whole package—someone to build a life with. Since Stephanie had her eyes on power and the penthouse suite, he had told himself from the get-go she was not *that girl*. But after seeing her with Brenda and Barbara, he knew the heart of a potential mom beat beneath the navy pinstripe she donned for work.

He had resigned himself to letting her go once her year-long stint was over. Now, things had changed. *Love* changed things. He needed a new plan.

Since she didn't know the area, he determined to show her all the things he loved about the place he called home. He worked harder to prove Paul Mason's guilt so she would know the value of having a cop in her back pocket. But when she remained on her chosen career path, Brett realized he needed a back-up plan.

He blew the dust off his master's thesis, knowing the degree would take him where he needed to go. A security firm provided one. Accepting the firm's offer would make his career portable enough that he could move along with the woman of his dreams. It was a compromise, but life was full of them.

STEPHANIE'S EYES narrowed at the sight of the forty suits who sat, wall-to-wall, in the president's conference room. They had gathered to hear George Watson, Space Tech's CEO, make a live address from Ohio and, despite John Sanders's assurances she had nothing to worry about, her stomach churned. She straightened the lapel of her navy pinstripe, slipped into her reserved front row seat and crossed legs that were, thank goodness, not shaking. The oversize monitor on the wall filled with static.

Once the opening remarks were dispensed with, the company leader singled her out.

"I expect you to terminate Paul Mason's employment as of 4:00 p.m. today. Make certain he is escorted off the premises. Are we clear on everything else?"

"Yes, sir." Her mouth felt so dry she could plant cactus in it but, with everyone staring at her, she had to look strong. She swallowed her anxiety and began the expected summary.

"Reimbursement for the…"

Admitting she knew the numbers by heart would only emphasize them. She pressed a stylus against her Black-Berry.

"…fourteen thousand, six hundred and fifty-three dollars he stole, plus four days paid vacation, will be recouped from the remainder of his retirement fund. If he refuses, Space Tech will press charges."

Not an option, according to the CEO. "It is your job to convince Mason to reimburse the company he defrauded. It's in his best interest."

Stephanie stifled a frown. The corporate office was counting on her to make the soon-to-be-ex security guard leave quietly to avoid bad publicity. That wouldn't sit well with Brett. He was convinced Paul Mason's sorry butt belonged in jail, but the decision had never been hers to make.

"Yes, sir," she said. "I'll take care of it."

George continued. Since an exhaustive audit had failed to uncover another single instance where an employee had abused the hurricane fund and the restructuring of the Florida office was ahead of schedule, she would stay on as head of HR. There was more good news—bonuses for her entire department, and extra time off as a reward for their part in the investigation—but Stephanie was too busy trying to corral a face-splitting grin to hear much of it.

She was staying put.

Staying put as in, "not recalled to the home office." As in "keeping her job." As in, given "time to build a life with the man she loved."

Her fingers drummed one thigh until the speech-making finally ground to a stop and the appropriate closing remarks were made. A month earlier, she would have turned cartwheels at the congratulatory handshakes offered by her peers. Today, she cut the compliments short. Citing a need to resolve things with Paul Mason, she bolted for the door at her first opportunity. But it wasn't the guard she was anxious to deal with. Her fingers fumbled for her cell phone while her stilettos threatened to dance their way down the hall.

"Brett, I just got out of the meeting," she said at the beep. "Everything went great! Better than great! I'll give you the details when I see you." She dropped all pretense to ask, "Are you looking forward to tonight? I am." A nice, relaxing evening with Brett was just what she needed after all the stress Paul Mason had brought into her life.

Okay, so *nice* and *relaxing* were not on the agenda.

She and Brett had had a month of nice and relaxing. Thanks to a high school buddy, Brett had taken her on a private tour of the Kennedy Space Center. They had watched stars from the planetarium at the local college. They had dined from Micco to Titusville and fished the St. Johns River from one end of the county to the other.

Finally, after a month of going everywhere else, the man she loved had invited her to his place. Her gait tightened at the thought of "pasta and whatever" with Brett. Her broad-shouldered Adonis had insisted he did not cook Italian, which was okay with her. She wasn't hungry. At least, not for food.

Tonight was all about the *whatever*. She'd given her heart to the tall, sexy cop that first day on the river. Tonight, she intended to give him the rest.

A thrill passed through her and she paused, her hand on her office doorknob. One last hurdle remained between where she stood and the evening she and Brett had planned. Only one, but it was a doozy. She had to fire Paul Mason.

The necessary paperwork sat on her desk. Her own office had been cleared, her staff sent on various assignments. Last, but not least, three burly guards on loan from another division waited just out of sight in case things turned ugly. She squelched the wave of bitterness that rose whenever she considered the man who had duped her, took a deep breath and punched numbers into her phone. Her voice dropped to the tone her staff had learned to respect.

"Send Paul Mason to my office immediately."

She could handle Paul Mason, she told herself. She could handle a dozen Paul Masons. It was the Brett Lincolns of the world who got to her.

THE LATEST from the Red Hot Chili Peppers blasted out of all nine Bose speakers as Brett pulled the Avalanche into a parking spot in front of Pat's Place. Whistling the rest of the song, he checked his image in the rearview mirror, smoothing his plaid shirt to hide his off-duty weapon. Satisfied, he hustled toward the door. He had just enough time to grab a couple of dogs before stopping at his favorite butcher shop. Then it was home to mow the lawn, take a quick shower and change, toss a salad and fire up the grill. Stephanie was due at eight, and he wanted everything to be perfect because…tonight was the night.

He had known she was "the one" their first date, at The Yellow Dog. She was everything he wanted—smart, funny, caring, and she packed more downright sexiness into her five-foot-two-inch frame than any woman he had ever known. Even though they hadn't made it as far as the bedroom, he was sure. Sure they would be good together. Pretty sure he loved her—oh, yeah. And tonight, unless he had totally misread the signals, they would take their relationship to the next level.

So they had only dated for a month. So what? And so the guys on the force thought she was cut from the same cloth as his previous girlfriends. Again, so what? Tom and Mary argued the other side and their vote counted for something, didn't it? He jingled his pocket change in time with the music.

"Hey, Sam. How're you doin'?"

"Veddy good, sir."

Brett scanned the store when his usual greeting failed to earn the owner's trademark white-toothed grin. Aisles of snacks and essentials were practically empty—just him, Sam and one other customer. The normal midafternoon lull. He shrugged aside a flash of concern.

"Kids okay?"

It seemed as if Sam or his wife was behind the counter of the convenience mart 24/7, yet they still managed to produce a new baby every year or two. He and Stephanie hadn't talked about children. If they made that long walk down the aisle, how many would they have? His steps slowed as he considered how much fun making them would be.

"Veddy good, sir."

With still no smile from Sam, the lone customer deserved a second look. Bulky windbreaker, dark. Jeans. Tennis shoes. The unfamiliar face beneath the baseball cap set off no alarms. He looked like a deliveryman, which explained the heavy jacket. Many of them plunged from ninety-degree heat into subzero freezers and back again, day in and day out.

It was an honest way to make a living, but he'd stick to police work.

Moving to the center aisle where hot dogs and sodas were self-serve, he wondered if Stephanie realized what being married to a cop was all about. She rarely saw him in uniform, but she had known what he was from the moment they met. The memory of their first encounter brought a smile to his lips even as he shook his head.

Their rocky start hadn't kept him from falling in love with her. Nor would his work keep them from building a life together. He grabbed a paper cup and held it under the ice tube. His reflection in the shiny metal soda dispenser outgrinned Sam's any day of the week.

Except there was no smile on Sam's face today.

The dark-skinned man wore a troubled look and, for the second time, Brett felt unease creep down his back. He pushed a button and listened to ice tumble into his cup while he watched the owner's reflection empty the contents of the cash register into a plastic bag.

Brett's pulse rate tripled. He slid sideways a half step to get a better view of the so-called customer when Sam handed the bag across the counter. The man in the jacket held his right arm crooked and stationary...and aimed at Sam.

Gun. Oh, shit.

Brett used the sound of soda pouring into the drip tray to cover the noise he made unholstering his off-duty weapon. Wishing he had told Stephanie he loved her, he waited while seconds stretched to hourlike proportions until the gunman took his first step toward the exit.

"Police! Freeze!" he shouted. With his next breath he added, "Get down, Sam!"

The thief spun, his gun hand swinging out.

Brett tasted copper. His vision narrowed to a tunnel. He stood at one end, the man with the gun at the other.

"Don't do it, buddy!" he yelled. The Glock felt enormous in his hands. He hoped it looked even bigger.

It must have because the gunman wisely froze.

Once the suspect was disarmed and down on the floor, Brett gulped air and yelled for Sam.

"Call for help," he instructed. "Tell Dispatch it's a Code 10-15, suspect in custody." His eyes glued to the would-be thief, he spotted tennis shoes—his own tennis shoes—in his peripheral vision. Brett kept his gun trained on the suspect while he wiped a dribble of sweat into his hair with his free hand.

"Be sure you tell them an off-duty officer made the arrest."

Being mistaken for an armed gunman would ruin his whole day.

He eyed the robber lying on the floor and sucked in a breath of air big enough to make his shoulders rise and fall. His vision cleared from freeze-frame images into a smoothly running track and, for the first time, he thought to check the parking lot where there was a decided lack of delivery trucks. He shook his head at the mistake only a rookie would make. What was he thinking, dropping his guard like that?

The instant replay showed he hadn't been thinking, at least not about the important things, the things that might get a guy killed.

He heard approaching sirens, followed closely by the sound of screeching tires. The parking lot filled with blue flashing lights, and uniformed officers poured into the store. Several quickly led the gunman to a patrol car.

After that, bedlam erupted. Everyone yelled or spoke at once, especially Sam. Babbling and gesturing wildly about the dangers of owning a business and the cop who had saved him, Sam was already on the phone providing his wife with a slightly exaggerated account of the event. It took four policemen to pry the grinning store owner from his corner behind the cash register. It took an act of Congress to get him off the phone long enough to give a statement.

Amid all the back-slapping, Brett's stomach suddenly lurched as if to remind him that taking down armed robbers was hard work and maybe he should eat something. The pair of hot dogs still sitting on the counter where he'd left them made him shudder. He'd never eat another one as long as he lived.

Which was a waste, considering Sam would probably give him a lifetime supply.

BY EIGHT O'CLOCK, Paul Mason was history and Brett was MIA. Above a carefully selected Chisato sundress and little else, Stephanie wore a troubled frown. Her stomach tightened as she listened to his doorbell echo through the townhouse. The charms of her favorite knockoffs clinked softly and the hem of her dress brushed her thighs while her weight shifted from one foot to another on Brett's front porch. She pushed the buzzer again.

No one came.

Had there been an accident? She had an instant image of him lying, hurt and alone, on some deserted stretch of road and shook her head. There were no deserted roads in Cocoa Beach. But their wires had gotten crossed somehow and she needed to find out why. Praying he had been called in to cover someone else's shift, was writing out speeding tickets or booking a suspect, she dialed the emergency phone number he had given her.

"This is Dispatch."

She dredged a name out of one of Brett's many stories. "Doris, this is Stephanie Bryant. We haven't met, but Officer Lincoln gave me your number. I wondered if I could speak to him. We were supposed to meet and—"

"Brett ain't on duty tonight, sugar."

"He's not?" Stephanie's heart sank to the toes of her faux–Jimmy Choos.

"He's down at Sticks N Tips celebratin' with the rest of my boys. You should join us there, honey."

Stephanie gave her cell a blank look, her grip on the phone tightening as relief that Brett was all right faded against feelings of betrayal. Her lower lip trembled until she bit it. She squelched the urge to vent by tapping her toes. The charms on her shoes jangled.

What next? she wondered when she had burned off enough anger and frustration to think clearly. It didn't take much imagination to predict Brett's reaction if she showed up at the bar dressed as she was. From the untamed curls he loved to plunge his fingers through, all the way down to her favorite come-and-get-me stilettos, she had dressed for one unmistakable purpose. Though tonight was so definitely *not* going to be the night, seeing her in the skimpy sundress would certainly teach him not to make the same mistake twice.

If he ever had to break another date, he would call first.

The lump of doubt in her throat refused to go away as she climbed back into her car. After the meeting with Corporate that morning, her first thought had been to share the good news with Brett. Yet here she was, a few hours later, driving to her least favorite place in Cocoa Beach because he had broken their Very Important Date in order to meet his cop buddies…and she had no idea what the boys in blue were celebrating.

Why hadn't he called?

The obvious reason, that he didn't take their relationship as seriously as she did, made her lip tremble again. She told herself she was lucky to find out now, before things had gone too far. But that didn't make her feel any better and with a resigned sigh, she drove through the drizzly rain to Sticks N Tips.

Stephanie threaded through the maze of haphazardly parked cars, carefully picking her way around shoe-ruinous puddles until she reached the bar's door. Inside, the party was in full swing. Heavy metal poured from overhead speakers. Conversation, punctuated every few seconds by raucous yells, buzzed beneath it. Before her eyes could adjust from bright sunshine to the sparsely lit interior, a vaguely familiar waitress shoved a fresh mug in her hands.

"Drinks are on the house, honey."

Judging from the yeasty smell of the place, beer flowed nonstop.

So many muscular men and sturdy women packed the room Stephanie wondered if any police were left to guard the city. The crowd made it impossible to elbow her way through without getting mauled or pinched or doused by someone else's drink. Since her revised plans for the evening included none of the above, she waited until she spotted a corner table where a hanging lamp spilled a pool of light onto a woman draped in a purple sari. Beside her sat a dark-skinned man Stephanie recognized from her morning coffee run. Even better, two empty chairs sat across from them.

Reaching for their names, she asked, "Ramya?" Her nod to the husband was more certain. "Sam. May I join you?"

"Ah, Ms. Stephanie. So good to see you. Please. Sit down."

"What are you doing here?" she asked. A cop bar seemed a strange place for store owners whose friendly service had wooed her away from the impersonal national chain across the street.

"You like my party, yes?" asked Sam.

"Your party? All this?" She waved a hand at an array of bar food on a nearby table. "Did you hit the Lotto or something?"

"In a manner of speaking," Sam answered. "My store was robbed and I was nearly killed today. To thank all the policemen who came to my rescue, I am having a party." When Ramya shuddered visibly, Sam wrapped his arm around her and drew her close.

"What?" Stephanie asked. She threw an irritated look over her shoulder. With all the racket going on in the back room, she could hardly hear what Sam was saying. "Are you all right?"

Patting his wife's arm, Sam answered. "Everything is, as you say, A-OK."

"Thanks to Officer Brett." Ramya's soft voice broke and fresh tears welled in her dark brown eyes. She appealed to her husband. "What if he had not stopped in when he did? Where would you be then?"

Sam hugged his wife, murmured into her ear. Stephanie waited until Ramya calmed before she interrupted.

"I'm sorry, but did you say Brett? Brett Lincoln?"

The couple nodded excitedly. "Yes! Yes!" they exclaimed. "Officer Brett!"

Sam gave Ramya a sideways look. When she nodded, he took over the explanation. "A thief robbed our store. He aimed a gun at me and stole all my money. He wanted more, and I think he would have shot me but your friend, Officer Brett, he pulled his gun and forced the robber to the ground. He saved my life."

Stephanie searched the store owner's face for a sign, but his earnest expression held no room for doubt. Still, he had to be mistaken. The man she loved would have called her if something so momentous, so dangerous, had happened to him.

Apparently not.

The clear tones of the bar bell rang out, instantly tamping down the noise level throughout the room. Stephanie held her breath as, along with everyone else, she swiveled to see the man of the hour emerge from the back room flanked by Jake and several other brothers-in-arms. A deafening shout greeted Brett's appearance. Amid high fives and enough back slaps to give a guy whiplash, his entourage began to inch its way through the room.

For two seconds, maybe less, Stephanie's heart thudded joyously as the group headed directly for her table. But two seconds, maybe less, was all it took before she realized that she was not the intended objective. Sam and Ramya were.

Of course they were. The crowd expected a show. Handshakes and praise, the more obsequious the better. Stephanie could almost hear each man playing his part. Sam, with his charming accent, honoring the bravery of the officer who had saved his life. And though he swaggered now more than usual, she could almost see Brett scuff his feet before succumbing to the crowd's demands to tell his story one more time.

She could not sit there and watch it happen. She eased from the table. Making her way past clumps of well-wishers, she added new phrases to her personal dictionary. Brett had performed a "takedown" according to one gushing fan. Funny, thought Stephanie, all she felt was a letdown. She splashed through puddles to her car while the heels of her shoes poked holes in her heart with every step.

Away from the music and the confusion of the crowded bar, she took a deep breath. It wasn't something they'd discussed, but she had known from day one that police work would place Brett in danger.

She got that.

She could live with knowing he placed his life on the line if, at the end of the day, he came home to the life they built together.

Brett had joined the force to help people. Even now, when the pressures of his work kept him from spending time with the very ones he wanted to protect and serve, he got up every day, dressed in his uniform, strapped his gun in its holster and walked out the door.

She respected that.

What she could not wrap her thoughts around was that he had chosen his cop buddies over her. He had come face-to-face with death that very day, but had he picked up the phone to tell her? No. Instead, he had raced off to celebrate with his pals on the force. What did that say about his feelings for her? If they did build a life together, was that what it would be like? Would she always come a distant second to his fellow officers?

She tried out several answers before deciding that every one of them doomed their relationship. Through a film of tears, she stared at the closed door of Sticks N Tips. Even though the neon sign in the window said OPEN, she knew better. The place was a cop bar where would-be lovers were oh-so-not invited. Behind those thick wooden doors, Brett had everyone who really mattered at his side.

Stephanie leaned against the headrest. Tears streamed from the corners of her eyes, dissolving any hope of building a life with the man who had stolen her heart.

ONE GLIMPSE of the amazingly hot Stephanie on her way out the door stopped Brett cold in his trek about the room. For the second time that day, he watched disaster unfold before him. This time, his blood turned to ice. Hoping no one would notice the way his hands shook, he thrust them deep into the pockets of his Dockers.

He should have called. He'd intended to.

All day, his plans for the night had refused to budge from one corner of his mind. But every time he'd reached for the phone, one of his fellow officers had slapped him on the back and demanded he rehash the whole story. Between that and the Review Board and meetings with the lieutenant, to say nothing of the reams of paperwork required whenever an officer—especially an off-duty officer—pulled his weapon, the day had simply gotten away from him.

But he'd never meant to put that hurt look on Stephanie's face. As scared as he had been in Pat's Place—he hadn't told a soul, but he'd literally been shaking in his Keds—he would rather face ten armed robbers than upset the woman he loved. And there was no doubt that she was upset. His stomach roiled as ominously as if he'd filled it with beer instead of soda.

Had he lost her?

Nah, he smiled tightly. He could still fix things. All he had to do was go after her, catch her in the parking lot and apologize. Imagining how they would kiss and make up was like applying a blowtorch to the ice in his veins. He stepped toward the door through which the love of his life had fled.

A hand on his shoulder pulled him back. He heard Jake's voice in his ear.

"Let her go, man."

Brett shook his head. "I messed up. We had a date and I—with all that happened today, I didn't call. She thinks I stood her up."

The older cop's fingers dug deep enough into Brett's shoulders that he gritted his teeth to keep from wincing.

"And I'm telling ya, let her go. You put your life on the line today, man, and this is your night. Any woman worth having would understand that. If she doesn't, it's because she's too self-centered to care about anyone but herself."

"You're wrong, Jake. And I need to fix this or I might lose her."

Jake leaned in so close Brett could smell every beer in the six-pack the man had downed and nearly every cigarette in the pack he had smoked.

"*You're* wrong," Jake growled. "You'll have to fix it later. Right now, there's a roomful of people waiting for you to make a speech and act like the hero you are. So buck up, boy-o. That little clothes horse of yours is gonna have to wait awhile."

Brett blinked until the room swam back into focus. He hated that Jake didn't approve of his girlfriend, but the senior patrolman was right about the hero part. With all the brass, his fellow officers and their assembled guests watching, he couldn't disappoint. The sooner he got this over with, the sooner he could straighten things out with Stephanie.

His heart wasn't in it, but he squared his shoulders anyway and put an extra ounce of swagger in his step. Cameras flashed and the room fell silent as he crossed it to receive the grateful thanks of Samraj and Ramya Patel. He endured another hour of back-slapping before making his escape.

On the short drive through Cocoa Beach, streetlights glowed with the brilliance of the diamond he hoped to one day slip on Stephanie's finger. Before he bounded from the SUV at her curb, Brett considered, and discarded, the idea of popping the question right away. A quick I'm-sorry-will-you-marry-me on her front porch would never do. The occasion deserved fireworks, something even more spectacular than the romantic evening he had planned at his place. The proposal would have to wait.

Brett grew shakier by the minute as he banged on Stephanie's door. After trying both her cell and home phones with no luck on either, he briefly contemplated breaking into her house before he remembered the over-look where they often ended their dates. The image of her at the railing soothed his fears. Picturing the onshore breeze ruffling her loose hair and tugging at the hem of the miniscule dress she had worn to Sticks N Tips, he loped toward the beach. Despite the dark velvet of a moonless night, he sped through the dunes. His heart racing, he skidded to a stop where the path opened up.

The lone figure on the wooden deck hid her curves beneath jeans and a bulky shirt, but Brett had explored enough of Stephanie's petite body for instant recognition to sizzle through him. He sucked in a relieved sigh that hitched when he caught sight of her bowed head and the way her hands clutched at her heart. She was crying.

The realization punched his gut and his breath released in a whoosh.

A sense of dread rushed in to fill the empty space. His mind warned him that this was more than a simple forgotten phone call while his heart longed to take her in his arms, tell her he was sorry and make everything all right again. He stepped onto the platform.

At once, Stephanie swung to face him, her arms falling to her sides.

"Go away, Brett."

Okay, he deserved that. After all, he had let her down. "Stephanie, honey. I'm sorry. Can you forgive me?"

Her voice thick with tears, she asked, "Do you know the only time you call me *honey* is when you've been to Sticks N Tips? I hate it."

"O-kay," he said slowly. He didn't have a clue where this was headed, but the show was all hers. He'd play along. "I won't call you *honey* anymore."

"That's all right." She shrugged. "It's over between us anyway."

The solid wooden rail behind him felt awfully good just then. Even though Brett knew she didn't mean the words the way they sounded, they jarred him. He reminded himself that no one called it quits over something so simple as a forgotten phone call. He hitched up his belt and prepared to grovel.

"Hon—Stephanie, I'm sorry. You're absolutely right to be mad at me. I should've called. I meant to. I wanted to. But things were so crazy—" He stopped himself before he ad-libbed his way into even more trouble. "I have no excuse. I should have called."

"Apology accepted."

Apology accepted. If that was true, why did he feel as if a sinkhole had opened beneath him and he was in danger of sliding to the bottom? He studied the small form huddled on the farside of the overlook.

"Don't we get to kiss and make up? They say that's the best part of an argument."

"No," she said simply. "It's over between us, Brett. I can't see you again."

Her words rushed him like a rising tide. Afraid he would drown, he drew back.

"Because I didn't call?" he asked incredulous. One ruined date was no reason for all this drama.

"Brett." She sighed and shook her head. "Did you remember my meeting at Space Tech this afternoon?"

Actually, the last nine hours had been so hectic he had forgotten the meeting she had spent the last month preparing for until she mentioned it. Thinking it best not to admit *that* fact, he realized she must have received bad news. He vowed to be supportive. "Stephanie, honey, it doesn't matter about your job. I make enough for both of us to live on till you find another one. We won't be rich or anything, but we can still be together."

She barked a short, bitter laugh. "The thing is, Brett, George loved the way I handled things. He's even giving me a bonus."

"Well, hey! That's great news!" He started across the deck to give her a congratulatory kiss. Her upheld hand stopped him.

"The point is, when I walked out of that room the only thing on my mind was you. I wanted to share the best news of my career…with you."

Brett thought back to the last time she had mentioned the meeting. It was scheduled for one o'clock, about the time he had pulled his weapon in Sam's store. He stifled a shiver. "I was a little busy right about then."

"My point exactly. My news wasn't earthshaking. No one was going to live or die because of it. But you—you faced down an armed gunman. You could have been killed. When it was over, what did you do? You headed off to a bar to celebrate with the people who matter in your life. So where does that leave me, Brett?"

"Stephanie, honey, I meant to call, but…"

"Please, Brett." Her voice whispered. "I asked you not to call me *honey*. You don't care enough about me to do that one little thing. I don't matter to you. You'll always choose your friends over me. Face it. The lowest member of the force means more to you than I do."

That wasn't true. It wasn't daydreaming about the guys on the force that had nearly gotten him killed that afternoon. But pointing that out would probably lead down a road he did not want to travel, and he sensed he was running out of time to head her off. He reached for a topic that would give them some breathing room.

"What about that guard? You going to let that guy get away with stealing money from your company because you don't want to see me?" It was weak, he knew, but his thoughts were all over the map. "We're still working on that, aren't we?" He knew the answer before he even saw her shake her head.

"Yeah, well, the guard is not an issue anymore. If you had returned my phone calls this afternoon, you'd already know that."

Despite the ocean breeze blowing steadily in his face, Brett could barely breathe. His arms crossed, he asked, "What are you talking about?"

"The CEO decided to let Mason off if he returned the money."

He knew thieves like he knew the back of his hand.

"He'll never do that," he scoffed. "Never in a million years."

"It's already done. Mason signed the papers in my office today. It's over, Brett. As finished as we are." Her voice sounded so dead, she might as well be delivering a eulogy.

Anger spiked his heart into overdrive. "And what did you get out of the deal? Another promotion?" When she refused to answer, he turned away.

Yelling at her wasn't going to patch the hole that threatened to drain all the good out of their relationship. If he was going to win her over, he had to be calm, to think rationally. He looked at the dark ocean.

The tide was nearly out. Usually, crabs and periwinkles played hide-and-seek among the shells that littered the exposed beach. On this moonless night, clouds obscured the stars. The swath of sand lay flat and black, as lifeless as his heart.

"You never intended to prosecute him, did you? You were just stringing me along until you got what you wanted. It was all about you from the very beginning, wasn't it?" he asked.

He was so deep into his own pain that he didn't see her blur past. When he finally turned, she was gone. Staring at the empty space where Stephanie had stood, Brett swallowed past his broken heart, hiked up his pride and headed for the one place where he knew he'd be welcome.

Chapter Ten

A quick trip to Ohio helped Stephanie survive the first brutal days after the breakup, but all too soon it was time to slap bandages over the empty space in her heart where Brett used to live, and get her head back into the game of climbing the corporate ladder. As soon as she sat in the kitchen where she and Brett had shared their first meal and their first kiss, she realized time alone would not heal her broken heart. So much of her experience in the Sunshine State revolved around the hunky but oh-so-full-of-himself cop, her heart would never mend until she filled the vacuum his absence created.

To do that, she needed a plan.

Unwilling to trust her life to random electrical circuits, she pushed her BlackBerry aside. Life plans deserved a permanent monument. With no stone or chisel handy, she settled for paper and pencil.

Keep your eye on the goal, she wrote at the top of the page. She had the skills to succeed as CEO. All she needed was time and a few lucky breaks. While she couldn't control the latter, with Brett out of the picture, she was swimming in the former.

"Look out, George," she whispered.

She would join a gym to exercise her body and take a class at the local college to exercise her mind. That still left some free time so, following her dad's advice, she jotted *Find a new boyfriend* at the bottom of her list.

Seeing the words in black and white made her stop to think. Her dad had advised her to get back on the horse, but what did he know? She was pretty sure the man had never been horseback riding. Maybe she should give her heart time to mend before she risked getting thrown again. She edged her V-neck shirt aside and took a peek. At the rate she was healing, she'd be whole in, oh, thirty or forty years. She drew a careful line through the last entry and added *Buy some new shirts* to her list. Her Florida wardrobe simply revealed too much.

For the next few weeks she concentrated on Step One, barreling through days that stretched long past midnight, until exhaustion finally sent her to bed where she managed a few restless hours before starting all over again. Through it all, her heart remained wounded and raw. Though the pain didn't ease, the long hours began to pay dividends.

Forty-two days and ten hours after the breakup, Stephanie stood at her office window absently watching the morning sky turn from pink to gold while her printer spat out a memo green-lighting her request for a company picnic. Knowing Corporate would never approve a hurricane party, she had sold the idea of a morale-boosting celebration to mark the end of a successful quarter. The home office was pleased with the idea, especially after she pointed out the good PR they could generate by including local charitable groups in the festivities. The picnic was the latest in what was quickly becoming a string of accomplishments and one she had lobbied hard for since John Sanders wanted it so badly.

"We have to do something for our family," insisted the man who had become her mentor.

Stephanie's brow furrowed and she propped one hand at the waistband of her narrow black skirt while she studied the list of local groups the home office wanted her to invite. There was at least one she didn't recognize. Hoping John could tell her what a PAL was, she hit his speed dial button and waited for the company founder's usual effusive greeting.

"Stephanie, what's up?" asked a gruff voice.

Okay, so she deserved the brush-off. The last time he had called, she was in a meeting. The time before that, she had had to cut their call short when Corporate buzzed in with third-quarter updates. It was no way to treat your mentor but, as he constantly reminded her, getting ahead meant staying on top. She expected that he, having been there and done that, would understand.

"John, I've just received some great news from the home office," she began. "That—"

"And I have news for you," he broke in. "We can swap stories over lunch. I'll make reservations at the Italian Courtyard."

Stephanie wrapped a strand of hair around one finger and gave it a sharp tug. Lunch was not on her agenda, but when the man in charge said, "Let's," you found a way, even when the restaurant he chose was closer to home than the office. Whatever her friend had to say, she hoped it was important enough to justify a meeting in such an inconvenient spot.

"Twelve-thirty sharp."

That last bit wasn't a request. "I'll be there," she said to a line that was already dead.

Shoving her irritation aside, she turned to the details of the picnic. The event for three thousand—employees, families and guests—had to be over-the-top fun. A difficult feat to pull off under any circumstances, it was even more so when the hard crust over her wounded heart made her apathetic toward practically everything. Despite her own feelings, she was determined to do a good job and by the time she pushed away from her desk at precisely twelve o'clock, most of the arrangements had been made.

"I'll be back at four," she reminded her secretary. "Everyone who volunteered to help with the picnic has been notified and assigned their tasks. I'll line up donations for door prizes and the like this afternoon. The only thing left is to invite the youth groups."

"Already on it," the efficient Ralinda answered. "Everyone but PAL has confirmed. I've left a message for their director."

PAL, the mystery group. Stephanie considered asking about it until the alarm on her BlackBerry sounded. If she didn't leave that minute, she'd be late for her lunch date. Not a good idea, considering John already sounded miffed. With a quick "Good job," she was out the door.

The scent of orange blossoms drifted in the breeze and Stephanie stretched, glad to be outside on a warm fall day. It was definitely better than watching the weather through the windows of her office, and she realized John might be on to something. A late lunch beneath trellised vines where the scent of garlic and oregano blended with salty ocean air—it might be just what the doctor ordered.

Or not…since John had requested a table indoors.

Once they were tucked into an alcove off the bustling main dining room where murals and twinkling lights defined the ambience, she expected the older gentleman to get right to the point. She was wrong. While Frank Sinatra crooned in the background, John kept the conversation light as he swirled shrimp and scallops through a fragrant marinara sauce. Stephanie did her best not to look antsy. She speared a piece of the grilled chicken in her Caesar salad and wished he'd get on with whatever had brought them there. Over tiramisu and cannoli, he finally did.

"What happened to that young man you were seeing?" John asked without preamble.

Thinking of Brett caused a familiar ache in her chest. She sank her spoon into the tiramisu and held it there so she wouldn't rub the sore spot. "We broke up." She couldn't help it if there was more vinegar in her answer than she wanted.

"Not seeing anyone new?"

She abandoned her spoon to the dessert plate and grabbed her water glass. Where was this conversation headed?

"No. No one," she answered. "Why do you ask?"

A cryptic smile played around the corners of John's mouth. "I don't mean to pry." He broke off a piece of cannoli before speaking again. "Well, I do. But for a good reason."

Stephanie stilled. If her mentor made a pass, it would ruin their relationship. She tightened her grip on the glass until her fingers ached.

Letting her hang, John sipped his coffee, settled the cup into his saucer and blotted his lips. Then he cleared his throat and beckoned her forward, clearly signaling his wish to share a secret.

"Space Tech is my family in more ways than you know."

Without interrupting, Stephanie let her eyes fill with questions while relief sighed over her lips. Whatever John wanted, his focus would always be on the business.

"My wife and I chose not to have children in order to give

birth to this company. She was the perfect helpmate, my Margaret. In the early days when I worked out of our garage, she was the company secretary and treasurer. After our first success, she entertained all the right people and maintained the right connections. As a result, we had thirty good years together. A bit too busy. Hmmph." He blinked watery eyes before continuing. "We looked forward to taking all those vacations we missed, told ourselves we'd get to it after I retired. But the time to step down never seemed quite right. And then she was gone, and those plans ended."

What did you say when a friend exposed the unexpected sorrow of his life? "I'm sorry," sounded too trite. "You must miss her terribly," Stephanie murmured.

John waved a dismissive hand. "Don't mind me," he said. "I'm just an old retired fogy with nothing to give except advice."

The remark called for an argument and Stephanie hurried to say, "You could never be that, John. The board of directors would welcome you back. Aren't you still a majority stock holder?"

He chuckled, clearly amused by her question. "Yes, I still have a fair share of stock in the company, but that's not the point." He cleared this throat. "This child of mine, Space Tech, is all grown up and has moved on. Like any father, I'm proud of it, but it doesn't need me anymore. And like any young adult, it would resent my trying to exert any real authority over it. No, it's time for Space Tech to have a younger, more vibrant leader at the helm."

Stephanie no longer needed a road map to know where John was taking the conversation. She scooped a bite of ladyfinger and relished the combination of rum and marsala as it slid down her throat. The rich tiramisu tasted like success.

"*You* could have a real influence on the company's future," John continued. "You've made all the right choices so far. Not developing a serious relationship while you were in Ohio. Breaking things off with that young police-man before he derailed your career. Tough choices, but you'll face tougher ones along the line. I have big plans for you, my dear. You have what it takes to become the first female corporate head of Space Tech."

Stephanie placed her spoon back on the saucer. Okay, so tiramisu wasn't quite as rewarding as she'd thought it would be, and John was seriously misinformed. True, she hadn't dated much during her four years at corporate head-quarters, but at the time she was living at her parents' where she could save every penny. Even if she had wanted to indulge in casual sex—*Not!*—bringing a date home was against the house rules.

Nor had she called it quits with Brett because he inter-fered with her career. Her ex-boyfriend was the one who valued job and friendships above their relationship, not the other way around.

John kept talking. Whether he was ignoring her discom-fort or didn't see it, she couldn't tell.

"Statistically, most marriages fail. You've done well to avoid it. And children are out of the question, of course. No matter what the glossy magazines say, the head of a major corporation can't have it all. The company has to be your family, like it was mine. I can't tell you how happy I am to find someone who shares my commitment to Space Tech." His speech-making done, he flashed a father's proud smile before he motioned for their check. "So, are you ready to pack your bags for your next assignment? How does Washington sound?"

Though she prided herself on being cool when problems

turned up the heat, Stephanie's teeth rattled against the cup as she gulped coffee. John made being groomed for leadership in a major corporation sound like taking vows and entering a nunnery.

Was that what she wanted? Not at the expense of a home and a family, she didn't. Unfortunately for her, she wanted it all with the one person who couldn't put her first in his life.

Beneath the table, her fingers drummed her thigh. Since she couldn't have the future she wanted with Brett, shouldn't she take what she could get?

She would have sworn the words "Thank you very much!" were on the tip of her tongue, so saying, "I'm going to need a few days to think this over," surprised her. "I hope you don't need my answer today."

"Perfect!" John chortled. He rubbed dry, age-spotted hands together greedily before clasping his fingers. "A good leader never rushes the important decisions. Take your time," he said with a conspiratorial wink. "I think you'll make a fine CEO one day."

Back at the car, Stephanie's thoughts were so jumbled she paid scant attention to the familiar yellow slip tucked under her windshield wiper. Crumpling the latest in a series of unwanted presents from various "Brett is my buddy" officers into a ball, she tossed it onto the backseat. John, however, did more than glance.

"Stephanie?" he asked with an incredulous look. "How's your driving record?" He hooked a thumb toward the rear of the car where a dozen or more paper balls littered the floor.

She felt laughter bubble up and clamped a stifling hand over her mouth. "Never date a cop," she said, forcing a light-hearted smile. "More to the point, don't break up with one."

John leaned on his cane and issued a warning. "A bad driving record could influence your career."

He had a point.

"Not a single moving violation since the day I got my license," she answered. "Lately, I've acquired enough warnings to paper a small room, but I tell you, it's made a better driver of me."

"Hmmph." John, apparently, didn't find humor in either her answer or the situation. "It reminds me of a young boy pulling a girl's pigtails to get her attention. Put an end to it."

"I'll put a stop to it today," she promised before the older man climbed into his own car.

As Stephanie watched Space Tech's founder drive off, she wondered if he could be on to something. Was Brett trying to get her attention? John's opinions to the contrary, she knew it was possible to balance home and family and a successful career. You just had to have the right man in the mix.

Was Brett that man?

She'd had her doubts there for a while, but if—as John suggested—Brett was trying to get her attention... She shivered despite the heat.

She would have to call. Not see him, no. One glimpse of his rugged good looks and powerful physique and she'd fall into his arms without asking a single question. And she had to do it before she lost her nerve.

Once she crossed the causeway on her way back to the office, Stephanie maneuvered between choppy blue water and the drooping magnolias that lined a narrow twisting road. She spun the wheel onto the first of several residential cut-throughs that ran between the river and busy US1. Only a block from sprawling riverfront parcels with their million-dollar minimansions, older homes sprouted primly from thick lawns divided by woody bougainvillea and hibiscus hedges. She hit the brakes in front of one with a For Sale sign in the yard.

Already her hands had grown so damp she was forced to rub them on her skirt. On the edge of losing her nerve, she whipped out her cell phone and punched the number she had been unable to forget. Her anxiety ratcheted up with every ring until one of her high-heeled feet drummed the floorboard while she waited for an answer.

By the fifth ring, she was certain she had missed her chance. She was just waiting for the beep so she could deliver her speech to voice mail when, with a click and a groan, Brett came on the line.

"Hul-lo. Lincoln here," said a voice that sounded as if it had spent all night in a smoky bar. Which was ridiculous, Stephanie knew. Despite the cigarette burns scarring its furniture, Sticks N Tips had gone smoke-free along with practically every other bar and restaurant in Florida.

"Brett," she said and then stopped, wondering if she needed to introduce herself.

"Stephanie?" The voice on the other end of the line sounded a lot more alert.

Hearing a loud creak and the flap of bedcovers being thrown back, she momentarily lost herself in the image of Brett's handsome form stretched out on his bed, a bed she had intended to share with him the night of their last date.

"Honey!"

If he hadn't ditched her to go to Sticks N Tips.

"Honey?"

If he hadn't accused her of using him.

"Brett, it's…" She checked her watch and nearly groaned. What was she doing, sitting in a hot car talking to the man who had broken her heart when she should be on her way back to the office? "It's nearly four. Did I wake you?"

"No, no, it's okay. I was getting up anyway."

In time for happy hour? They both should have left their drink-all-night-sleep-all-day years far behind. Apparently, only one of them had.

She choked back a sharp "What on earth are you doing in bed in the middle of the day?" and replaced it with an "I didn't mean to disturb you" that carried only a slightly irritated edge.

"Stephanie, honey. It's okay," he said. "I worked a double shift last night so one of the guys could go to some function at his kid's school, but I have to be…somewhere…in a little while."

As if to prove he was telling the truth, she heard an alarm sound through the receiver.

"Oh, he— Hold on." There was another heart-wrenching rumble of mattress noise before the loud buzz shut off abruptly. "Now, what is it?"

"I, uh…" *I love you and I want to have your babies.*

No, she couldn't say that. Calling her "honey" proved he had been spending time at Sticks N Tips. The leopard had not changed his spots.

Angry and disappointed tears stung her eyes and she scrubbed furiously at them. Why had she even bothered? He might be trying to get her attention, but she would always take second place to his pals on the force. Even Space Tech thought she deserved better than that. They wanted to make her numero uno, didn't they? Firming her voice along with her resolve, she began again.

"I've accumulated quite a few tickets lately and—"

"You want me to fix them? Oh." Brett's voice dropped so low she knew the idea disgusted him. "I don't even get a break with those. Sorry."

"No, that's not what I meant." She hurried to correct his

impression before he decided she was a total loser. The limit on those was one per relationship and they had already met their quota. "I've gotten a number of *undeserved* tickets. Warnings, actually. For the most trivial things. It's beginning to feel rather, um, calculated." She inhaled deeply. "I'd like you to stop."

No longer disgusted, his voice filled with anger. "You're accusing me of plastering your car with paper?"

She had to prove that she could give as good as she got. "Maybe not you personally," she shot back, "but it started the day after we broke up and I don't have any other enemies on the police force. So how long do you and the boys in blue intend to harass me?"

Brett didn't answer for so long she was sure he had hung up on her.

"Brett. Are you there?" she demanded.

"Yeah, I'm here." They were back to disgust, but at least the anger had faded. "Look, whatever you're thinking, you're smarter than this. I can't believe you'd accuse me of some grand conspiracy just because you got a couple of parking tickets."

"Not tickets. Warnings," she said, trying for patience. "Twenty-two. No, make that twenty-three. I got another one today at the Courtyard."

"Twenty-three?" She nearly felt the whoosh of air Brett breathed into the phone. "Okay, you're right. Something's going on."

"So can you stop? Please?"

"It's not me, but I'll take care of it."

She didn't know whether to believe him or not. Either way, she deserved a better answer. "If you're not doing this to me, Brett, who is? And why?"

"I don't know," he said simply. "The guys never did

anything like this when I broke it off with—" His voice faded briefly. "But, hey," he said in a rush, "let me see if I can work it out. It might take a day or two. Will you give me a chance?"

The question was so leading it tempted her to confess how willing she was to give him a chance on every front, but just then her cell phone buzzed and danced in her hand before emitting a series of loud chirps. Saved by the bell, she thought grimly. She had been on the verge of embarrassing herself. A quick glance told her the incoming call was from her office. "I need to take this. Can you hold on a second?"

But Brett was apparently in a hurry to get off the phone. "Don't worry about it. I have to get moving here anyway. I'll be in touch."

For the second time that day, Stephanie listened to dead air. In disbelief, she blinked back the tears that stung her eyes and blurred the display on her cell phone. *Call Ended.* Of all the nerve. She snapped the device closed, electing to leave Ralinda to handle whatever crisis had prompted the interruption. She had a crisis of her own to deal with.

As far as kiss-and-make-up sessions went, distance had robbed them of the kissing part, and there had been decidedly little making up. Brett hadn't been trying to get her attention. He hadn't even known about the tickets. Which made her sound like an idiot for accusing him of such a juvenile prank. She tossed her cell phone onto the seat beside her and hit the steering wheel hard enough that it would have brought tears to her eyes if they hadn't already been there.

She wanted to be over him. She needed to be over him.

Instead, she knew the hole in her wounded heart had reopened. Leaning her head onto the headrest, she closed her eyes and made no effort to staunch the hot tears that seeped between her lids.

Unlike the river she had shed over Brett in recent weeks, the tears she cried in the car beneath a wide magnolia tree must have possessed oddly curative powers. As she blew her nose and blotted her cheeks she thought it might finally be over between them. She tested the waters by envisioning a life without the hunky cop and found that all the pain and sorrow she had carted around with her for weeks had been washed away. In its place lay a new certainty about what she wanted in life and how she was going to get it. Okay, so maybe there was just a wee little bit of anger tucked down in one corner of her heart, but she knew how to get rid of that, too.

Retrieving her cell phone, she scrolled through the address book to find the number she wanted.

"Deb, I need you to do something for me," she said as soon as the Realtor came on the line. "Remember when you said hurricanes don't come ashore in Cocoa Beach? Well, they do, and, apparently, one nearly demolished the house you sold Space Tech."

"That wasn't a hurricane," Deb said, sounding smug. "It was a tropical storm."

"Big diff. The fact remains, the house was practically destroyed."

"Yes, but…" Deb sputtered, "the owners rebuilt it."

"You still had an obligation to disclose. And you failed to do so." She paused long enough to register Deb's sigh before she offered an olive branch.

"In exchange for overlooking that fact, I need you to round up door prizes and gifts for the youth groups we're hosting at a company picnic in two weeks. Two or three thousand dollars' worth should do the trick."

"Are you insane?" Deb asked. "That's way too much."

Stephanie muffled a snicker at the apoplectic look the

tall thin blonde was almost certainly wearing. Then, as if it were of no consequence at all, she tossed out her most convincing argument. "Why, Deb, I thought you'd welcome the opportunity to support your community. Especially since it means I won't file a complaint with the Board of Realtors."

"Ever?" Deb bargained.

"Ever," she agreed. "Thanks so much. I knew I could count on you."

This time, someone else listened to dead air while Stephanie searched her heart. Just as she had suspected, she had poured out the last of her anger.

There was one more call she needed to make but, with the workday nearly over, she decided to skip it. Telling John that as much as she appreciated the fast-track offer to the penthouse suite, she would have to pass, well, that could wait till another day.

Are you sure?

Stephanie asked the question a final time while an unconditional *Yes* echoed through her body. If nothing else, her willingness to chuck her career over a marginal chance to reunite with Brett had taught her one thing—she did not have the commitment Space Tech required for climbing its corporate ladder. Not only that, she had begun to think of her little house on the beach as home. She wanted to make it a permanent one. With or without a certain hunky cop.

At the foot of the causeway leading from the mainland to Cocoa Beach, she slowed long enough to watch a man wade the river with two young boys. The trio carried fly-fishing equipment and the sight momentarily stole her breath. Once she had dreamed of children who would share Brett's love of the outdoors, but those dreams had died along with their relationship.

Though the thought sent a wave of pain and sadness washing over her, she reminded herself that bitterness came from dwelling on lost loves and lost opportunities. It was time to move forward. After one last look at the river, she headed home.

Chapter Eleven

Brett settled back onto the mattress, his hands folded behind his head, and let a low whistle ride his first full breath in six weeks. Ever since that night on the beach he had been as jumpy as a two-pack-a-day guy gone cold turkey, but no more because…she had finally called.

So what if she hadn't apologized. Apologies were overrated.

So what if she hadn't begged for a second chance. She was going to get one whether she begged for it or not.

So what if the best excuse she could drum up was some lame story about too many traffic violations. What did he care? She was still interested, that was the important thing. Her phone call dared him to make a go of their relationship and, this time, he was up to the challenge. Hadn't he spent the last month and a half preparing for this very moment?

Not entirely.

He had to admit he'd spent that first week wallowing in Broken Heartsville. He'd probably still be there if Fate, in the form of his best friend's wife and two little munchkins, hadn't intervened. A week after the breakup, he'd been standing in the back of the line at a fast-food place when a couple of future Miss Americas had nearly tackled him to the ground. He'd tried to dodge Mary's searching look, but twin cries of "Unca Brett, where's my present?" had distracted him. Before he could say "Some other time, maybe," he had a date—orders, really—to go fishing with Tom.

It still took a pair of waders to make him talk.

Before sunrise the very next day, he and Tom plied the shoreline in acceptable manly silence. They were listening for the telltale splashes of something big feeding in the shallows when Brett looked up to see a rod-and-reeler stepping to the river's edge. Tom issued an amused "Tourist!" at the sight of waders that looked like bib overalls. After Brett chimed in with "Snowbird," they sloshed their way to the ill-informed newcomer where they educated the man about the dangers of wearing chest waders in a river pocked by deep dredge holes. Bob-from-New-England was soon headed for shore with the business card of a local guide in his hand, but worry so consumed Brett he forgot himself and spoke out loud.

"You don't think Stephanie would make a dumb mistake like that, do you?"

The question landed a sharp look from his friend. "Does she even fish?"

"I took her. Some." To keep his hands busy, he stripped backing off his reel and spun it on again. "If she orders equipment online, she might buy waders. Most catalogs show fly fishermen wearing 'em."

Tom shrugged, a tough thing to pull off when whipping fly line back and forth through the air. "Just tell her not to."

"Can't. We're not talking."

With that, Tom's loop collapsed. His fly made a noisy splash as it landed somewhere behind him.

"You broke up?"

Brett nodded without trying to hide his misery. He felt the rising sun illuminate every hair on his unshaved face while his best friend scoured him with the same searching look Mary had used in the restaurant.

"What happened?" Tom asked. Proving his worth as a friend, he took Brett's raised shoulders for an answer and shook his head. "If I didn't have Mary…"

Brett fumbled his rod, nearly dropping it into the water at his feet.

"You love her?" Tom asked with his next cast.

"Yeah." Brett whipped his own line through the air to cover his embarrassment.

"You're terminal. You might as well get down on your knees and beg for another chance." This time Tom's line sailed true and his fly landed without creating a ripple beneath the weeds along the shore. "But I'd straighten up my act if I were you."

Only a best friend could say something like that and get away with it. Pretending he had spooled it on unevenly, Brett stripped line from his reel until he reached the solid metal core that anchored everything together.

"You gonna fish or stand there all day?" Tom finally asked.

"Fish," Brett answered, smoothly reeling in his line. He kept "And make some changes" to a whispered mutter.

"You're toast, y'know," his friend jibed. "You'll never have a moment's peace till you make it right with her." He waited a beat before adding, "Not that you'll have much peace after that."

The laughter of both men rang out over the wide, still water.

WHEN HE'D TAKEN TIME to think about it, Brett had realized two of the three people he trusted most had told him he needed to make changes in his life. And after weighing the advice he'd been given, he'd made a real effort to do just that. As his first step, he'd cut out the whole bar scene. Instead of heading to Sticks N Tips to lift a few cold ones after each shift, he'd begun heading for the gym where he lifted cold steel.

He had run the beach, his feet pounding the sand until the only thing he could think about was drawing his next breath. He'd run until sweat lathered his skin as if he were a winded horse. It didn't help. When he would look up, a woman who could pass for Stephanie's twin would be gathering shells in the pools left by the receding tide. She'd be browsing among the mom-and-pop shops in downtown Cocoa Beach. She'd haunt his dreams.

Man, was she ever in his dreams.

Remembering their conversation in her kitchen that first night—before the kiss that had tilted his world on end—he'd recalled what she said about getting involved and paying back. He had blown off her advice then, but when the chief posted a bulletin announcing the Police Athletic League was looking for volunteers, he was the first to sign up.

Brett grinned and shook his head. Stephanie probably wouldn't believe it if he told her how much fulfillment his two "little brothers" brought to his life. Nine-year-old Jimmy challenged him every step of the way. Brett liked the kid's spunk, even though the chip he carted around sometimes landed him in trouble. Only two years younger, Joey was altogether different. The little boy was afraid of anything new. Brett had determined to break through to both of them. He thought he was making progress.

To his amazement, the brothers had been leery of getting their feet wet. Brett couldn't imagine growing up in Florida and never wading the creeks or rivers. But after a few fishing trips, the boys had gotten the hang of it and started to enjoy themselves. They were even mastering the art of fly fishing despite having to use Brett's hand-me-down rods, a situation he hoped to correct in time for an upcoming fishing tourney and picnic.

Brett ran a hand through unruly, bed-head hair and stretched. Yes, he'd made changes. But there were some areas where a man couldn't compromise and still be true to himself, so he had refused to call Stephanie or apologize. Unfortunately, Stephanie was just as stubborn, so the stalemate had dragged on.

With every night that passed, it had taken more and more effort not to pick up the phone, but—finally—he had outlasted her.

The clock was ticking, though. If he was going to make things right with Stephanie before her year in Florida was up, he'd have to get started. Her lame excuse for a phone call made it easier, and he gave a half laugh.

Traffic tickets. She couldn't come up with something better than that?

Oh, he'd look into them all right. No doubt she had accumulated one or two, but no one could amass—what was it, twenty-three?—twenty-three tickets in six weeks without becoming the talk of Sticks N Tips.

Sticks N Tips.

Brett rubbed a hand over his unshaven face as he realized he hadn't visited the cop bar since his talk with Tom. A glance at his alarm clock told him his short foray down memory lane had put him behind schedule. A stop at the watering hole to check out the pool-table talk would have to wait until after his community service gig.

Whistling, he headed out to pick up the boys—his boys—at the PAL center.

THE SMELL OF STALE AIR and beer hit Brett square in the chest as he threw open the door to Sticks N Tips. When he'd been the new kid on the force, the place had possessed an allure far beyond that of worn chairs and tables that wobbled no matter how many folded matchbook covers were propped under the shortest legs. As his reputation had grown under Jake's tutelage, the bar's idiosyncrasies had become as familiar as the scar on his left thumb—the one he had sliced open building a model airplane with Tom when they were in the fifth grade. In time, he had learned how to bank shots off the left rail of the pool table so he missed the torn felt, how to rock the pinball machine just enough to guide the ball to the inlanes without going tilt. He could name every cigarette burn on the bar after two years. After three, he added the tables.

Weeks away from his old home away from home gave a different perspective. He had changed while Sticks N Tips remained the same—a hangout for guys who didn't have a life to go home to at the end of the day. Brett tightened his smile and squared his shoulders. He stepped into a world that, by choice, was no longer his.

"Hey, look who decided to pay us a visit."

Jake spoke to Mac, who was wiping down the long wooden bar. Last call was only minutes away and the place had emptied.

"It's about time, bro."

Experience told Brett that Jake had come there straight from work and had been drinking steadily. Waving off Mac's offer of a draught, he accepted a sloppy handshake from the senior cop and pulled up a chair.

"How you been, Jake? And how's—" He stopped. For the life of him, he couldn't remember the latest in Jake's string of three-month stands.

"Becca," Jake provided. "She's gone to visit her sister."

Brett nodded. Another relationship had run its course.

"So, hey. That was some takedown at Patel's, wasn't it? Just the way I taught—"

Brett eyed the third most influential person in his life and tried to look past the fact that the man was stone-drunk. "Yeah. I'm not here to swap stories. Jake, I got a little problem."

There was nothing the older officer liked better than to have his boys come to him with their problems. Jake straightened until his sprawl was moderately upright.

"Whazzup?"

"You remember that girl I was seeing? I introduced you one night."

"Steffie," grunted the man who, when cold sober, was brilliant and dead-on. He aimed a finger that missed the mark when his elbow slipped off the table edge. "You gotta break that cycle, man. She's just another round from the same chamber as your last gal."

The advice did not deserve a response and Brett didn't give it one. "I'm not here to discuss my love life. I came here because someone on the force has targeted Stephanie. She's gotten a slew of tickets in the last few weeks. She thought I was behind them and called to tell me to knock it off."

Deny everything was the standard reaction to any accusation against a fellow officer. Expecting his friend to reject Stephanie's claims, Brett's stomach lurched when Jake's mouth twisted into a wicked grin.

"She did, did she?" He drained the last of his beer and thunked the empty mug onto the table. "Hey, Mac. I need another one."

"Last call," growled the retired cop from Jersey. "How about you, Brett?"

"I'll pass, thanks," he told the bar owner before facing his one-time mentor again. "Tell me you're not behind this."

"Don't get bent out of shape. Her record's spotless."

True enough. Doris had pulled the info for him that afternoon. The only way Jake would know it, though, was if he…

Brett waited until Mac settled two beers, one ordered and one not, between them on the scarred table.

"Jake, buddy," he said after the owner moved out of range, "you gotta cut this out. The department'll come down all over you."

"Hey, man!" Jake raised his hands in mock innocence. "I never signed a single one o' them warnings. It's her word against mine. Who's gonna tell?"

Brett let his features stiffen into his game face. Anyone who made him choose between himself and the woman he loved was going to face severe disappointment. He felt Jake's eyes on him, saw them widen in disbelief.

"So. It's like that, izzit?"

Outlasting Jake's weak stare was no problem. "It's like that."

"She's just another self-cent—"

Brett growled his final warning. "That's my girl you're talking about. I don't want to hear another word against her. And if she gets so much as one—"

"I gotcha." One of the things that made Jake a good officer was his ability to know when to surrender the field. He sprawled in his chair, one arm spread across the torn leather of the empty seat beside him. He raised his mug. "Here's to the brotherhood. Let nothing divide us."

Brett stared down at the beer he had not ordered.

"You're not drinking," Jake prodded.

"Nah," Brett answered. "I've had enough." Jake and

the others like him were as much a part of his past as Stephanie was his future.

"Time to lock up," Mac interrupted.

Jake lurched to his feet. "Guess we'll finish that beer next time." Plunging his hand into his pocket, he missed and his fingers slid down his pants leg. As quickly as a drunk could, he made another stab, this time coming up with the desired keys.

Brett looked around the bar. There was no one else to drive the training officer home, and Jake was too drunk to walk, much less slide behind the wheel.

"Hey, man." He sidled up beside his superior. "Gimme your keys. I'll drive."

"Nah, I can manage. Izz only a cuppa' miles."

Brett required less than a split second to weigh the penalty for confronting his senior officer versus having one of CB's own pulled over for DUI. Or worse. He snagged the keys.

"You can call a cab or I'm driving. Your choice."

"Cab," Jake spit. "I ain't ridin' with you."

Mac had the local taxi company on speed dial and used it. Minutes later, Brett poured the man he'd once referred to as the finest cop he had ever known into the backseat. He gave directions to the driver and leaned against the bar's brick facade.

"There but for the grace of a good woman, go I," he murmured.

He had the right woman. Now, he just needed to win her over. And he had a pretty good idea how he was going to do it.

ACCORDING TO A GUARD who was not named Mason, Stephanie's door was at the end of the hall. Brett strode down the wide corridor on the third floor of the administration building, the freshly polished black shoes beneath his uniform squeaking against gleaming marble. He had always imagined his girl sharing a cramped space similar to his in the squad room, but his perception shifted upward as he passed the handsome selection of oils and watercolors on the walls.

Knowing he could have nearly the same thing if he wanted it helped him squelch a ripple of envy. Once he completed that master's thesis, one "Yes" to any number of recruiters would put him behind an executive desk in his own corner office of a private security firm. With his background in the Marines and on the CBPD, he had all the right credentials for the top job. Not that he was in a hurry to turn in his badge. He liked police work and took pride in what he did. He looked down the long corridor a second time, his chest swelling with admiration for his girl.

At the end of the hall, he paused to let his expectations climb another notch. Stephanie had never mentioned a *suite* of offices. The pound of chocolate-covered potato chips he meant as a peace offering suddenly seemed too paltry. Next time, he would splurge on the largest box of their favorite treat.

His glance took in a brass plaque mounted on the wall. Human Resources, it read, with Stephanie Bryant, Director, in only slightly smaller script below.

He took in the airy waiting room and the four adjacent office doors, all closed. The computer screen atop the mahogany reception desk had gone dark. The phone's Call Forward button blinked continuously. He stood wondering where everyone was until a slim blonde eased out of the office at the far end of the quad. She lingered at the closed door, her troubled expression straightening Brett's posture and compelling him to make another sweep of the office space. Though nothing looked out of the ordinary and only the soft buzz and hum of office equipment reached his ears, he had learned a valuable lesson at Pat's Place and no longer let his guard down.

Across the room, the frowning girl glanced up. "Oh!" she said, starting visibly. Her expression quickly changed from upset to curious. With a soft rustle of linen and silk, she glided toward him on a fresh wave of flowery perfume. "Is there a problem, Officer?"

Brett reached into his bag of tricks and dusted off a smile—the one Doris claimed could melt polar ice caps. It never hurt to have the secretary on your side.

"Hey. No problem. I'm not here on official duty." Extending a hand, he said, "I'm Brett Lincoln."

Apparently his name didn't register with the girl because her long, thin fingers slipped into and out of his grasp while the expression on her face never wavered. Which was okay, he told himself. He was almost thankful that Stephanie didn't talk about her personal life at work.

"I just dropped by to see St—Ms. Bryant. If she's available?"

Puzzlement flashed across the girl's face like a lightning strike. "I'm sorry, Officer Lincoln. She's in a meeting with—" She caught herself and threw a troubled look at the door she had just exited. "She's in a meeting," she repeated before she slid into the desk chair and swiveled to face him. "Would you like an appointment?"

"No thanks, Ralinda," he said with a quick look at the flustered blonde's badge. It took a little more effort than he expected to turn up the wattage on his smile. "Do you think she'll be free soon?"

"This might take a while," came a quick warning. "But

you could wait if you'd like." The secretary waved a free hand toward one of two comfortable-looking chairs. "Excuse me," she apologized as she brushed a piece of hair behind one ear to expose a wireless mike. With her voice pitched so low Brett almost couldn't hear it, she said, "Shelly, I'm back." She paused briefly, then, "No calls? Okay, thanks. I'll get back to you."

Ralinda pushed a button on the telephone, waited a second and said, "Human Resources. This is Ralinda. How may I help you?"

Being summarily dismissed wasn't something Brett was used to, but he made for one of the indicated chairs and settled in to wait. Ralinda's nails tapped her keyboard and she answered the occasional call in a monotone that quickly faded into the background while Brett fought boredom by flipping absently through one of several brochures touting Space Tech this and Space Tech that. He'd never really grasped how big the company was.

He fought the urge to look up when he heard Ralinda's voice drop to a conspiratorial whisper.

"Shelly, I'm telling you, it's true—she's leaving. I heard it myself when I delivered their coffee."

Brett flipped a page in the glossy advertisement and pretended an article about Space Tech's net worth and stock options was so engrossing he couldn't put it down.

"No, she's not like that. It's John. He's old school. Wants his coffee. You don't say 'No' to the company founder."

Brett thumbed to the inside cover where a caption identified a hawkeyed man as Space Tech's founder, John Sanders.

"Of course she'll take it. Who would turn down a huge promotion like that? What? Oh. Director of operations in Washington, D.C. She'll be in charge of the whole site—

Security, HR, Admin. It's huge, especially for a woman. She'll break that glass ceiling into a million pieces."

Ralinda must have realized that her voice had risen because, at the outer edge of his peripheral vision, Brett saw her aim a glance his way. Casually, he recrossed his legs, throwing the secretary an apologetic smile for the creak and groan of his leather holster. Exchanging one glossy print ad for another, he hoped Ralinda bought his act. She must have. Though she lowered her voice slightly, Brett had no trouble hearing half the conversation.

"Do you think? Oh, I wish. I've always wanted to live in Washington."

Ralinda nodded and listened while Shelly said something. After a short break she said, "Yes, she's a good boss. She's only been here a couple of months, but I'll miss her. She's really great."

Brett thought Stephanie was really great, too. Evidently, she was going to be really great somewhere else.

If a perp had gut-kicked him, the pain couldn't have been worse. Brett wasn't certain how he made it to his feet or out the door. He vaguely remembered a stop at Ralinda's desk where he'd said he'd catch up with Ms. Bryant some other time. He couldn't recall much of the twenty-four hours that followed.

Two weeks later, his pay stub showed a draw on his sick leave so he knew he must have called in. He could never swear to it in court, though. He didn't even know how he'd made it home. In fact, there were only two things he knew for sure about that day.

First, that he had been wrong about the time. He had convinced himself that he and Stephanie still had plenty of time to work things out. But their hourglass had run out of sand the moment she accepted a transfer to Washington without even considering him.

And that second thing? Oh, yeah.

Never—ever—leave a box of chocolates in a closed car in Florida.

Chapter Twelve

"Twenty-seven, twenty-eight, twenty-nine…"

Stephanie wrote the tally on her clipboard as laughing, excited picnic-goers disembarked onto the sandy beach from the white PAL bus. Faced with a small mob of impatient children and their enthusiastic chaperones, the lengthy welcome she had rehearsed degenerated into, "Glad you're here. Check in at the registration tables." She threw a wave in their general direction, and watched her guests hurry off, eager to enjoy the rides and games.

Left to wait for a couple of stragglers, she took a deep breath of salty air and eyed the shoreline where white birds soared high on thermals off the warm Atlantic. A fall weather system provided cloudless skies, but forecasts called for a late-season storm by the time afternoon rolled into evening. She made a note to keep one eye on the weather…and another on everything else.

It was, after all, her party. Even if she had little more to do than make a speech and measure the fish in the fishing tourney. She wasn't sure which of the staff had nominated her for that pleasant chore—probably someone who thought a city girl from Ohio would know nothing about fish—but the surprise was on them. Thanks to the man she had loved and lost, she knew a thing or two about fishing.

She waited for the expected tears and when they did not appear, ran a hand over hair she had slicked and tamed into a ponytail. The old adage about time and wounds really did work. She no longer ran to the ladies' room for a good cry every time thoughts of a certain cop crossed her mind. Sure, she still had the occasional bad day when she felt Brett's loss like a missing limb and mourned his decision to choose his pals over their relationship. But as time went on, she had more days like this one, where she could even picture them bumping into each other on the street and casually exchanging chitchat the way old lovers did in countless country songs.

It could happen. Maybe not for a million years, but it gave her something to look forward to. A girl needed that, didn't she?

A scramble of young feet made her shove her dreams back into the deep freeze where they belonged. She propped up a drooping smile and swung to face the yawning mouth of the bus where the tip of a long, thin rod appeared. It was followed closely by a grade-schooler who took extreme care not to bend or break the slender graphite. Each participant in the fishing derby would receive a pole and tackle box, courtesy of a generous donation from Tom's Marina, but these lingerers carried their own. And they were exceptional, she noted as the last two boys tromped off the bus.

"So, you're fly fishermen, are you?" The older boy stood with a cocked hip and a smirk that made him look a whole lot cuter than he probably intended while the little one beamed a wide, toothy grin her way. "Which one of you is going to win today's contest?"

The youngest gave an oddly endearing shrug before

he thrust his fly rod forward. "Like it?" he asked. "It's cool, ain't it?"

"Very cool," Stephanie managed, staring down at a smaller version of the rod she had used fishing with Brett. She hefted the cork grip, tilting the pole instinctively so the finish caught the glinting sun and turned brilliant. Why, of all the colors in the world, did these have to be that same incandescent green? With trembling fingers, she handed the rod back to its owner.

"He made 'em. For my brother an' me."

The smirker nodded over his shoulder just as two long legs swung into the dark stairwell of the bus. Sounds from the beach faded and Stephanie's world telescoped onto the doorway. Her eyes slid up a pair of rapidly appearing muscular thighs, sped past a trim waist and landed on shoulders broad enough to carry the world.

"I'm over him," she breathed.

Good ole Sol disagreed. The sun dropped a fraction lower, sending a shaft of light into the dark hollow, illuminating the strong jaw and bright blue eyes she saw in her dreams almost every night. The sight stole her breath.

"Brett." She nodded. She didn't know where the cool, polite voice came from. It certainly wasn't hers. Hers would squeak and ride up and down on her thudding heartbeat.

"Stephanie."

That Brett would show up chaperoning two young boys was so far off her radar it wasn't even a blip. She mustered as much nonchalance as an aching heart would allow and tightened her grip on the clipboard so she wouldn't fly into his arms. Such a move would only lead to more heartbreak, and she did not want to get burned again. She took a breath, hoping to calm her racing pulse.

"Didn't expect to see you here." The understatement of the year quivered so much that she sharpened her tone in self-defense. "Get roped into volunteering?"

"Back off, sister," piped the older kid.

Brett settled one hand on his shoulder. "Remember your manners, Jimmy," he said softly. "We talked about that."

The boy scuffed a foot through the sand in a motion too like Brett's to be coincidental. "Sorry," the child mumbled.

"I've been working with PAL for a while now," Brett said.

Long enough to build each of the boys his own fly rod, Stephanie realized, the earlier comment making more sense. She turned aside, aiming a quick look at the bus where someone had used teal spray paint to write Police Athletic League against the white background. PAL, the mystery group. Knowing she should have guessed, she felt her face redden.

"I'm sorry, too," she said. She had a number of regrets—none bigger than her breakup with Brett.

"Hey, we're okay. Aren't we, boys?" Brett's jaw worked. "Jimmy, Joey, this is Ms. Bryant. And this—" he waved a hand "—is her shindig. Looks like a great one, doesn't it?"

From the way his eyes roamed over her when he didn't think she was looking, Brett plainly meant more than the cookout. The boys, however, took his words literally. They quickly scanned the carnival-like atmosphere, their mouths gaping open when they spotted the food pavilion where a battalion of volunteers flipped burgers and stirred onions and peppers on massive steel grills.

"I'm hungry." Joey tugged the hem of Brett's white Polo until the teal-blue PAL insignia dipped.

"Okay, man," Brett said agreeably.

The older boy kicked a little sand. "I could eat," he announced.

Joey elbowed his brother. "I want to go on the rides."

Brett lifted his shoulders in an offhand way. "We'll do it all," he assured the boys before turning up the wattage on a smile so bright it blinded Stephanie no matter where she looked. "They just want to have fun. See you around."

"See you," she mouthed. The trio moved off, leaving her to stare after them. Breathless and hungry for something that was not cooking on the grills, she studied the crowd of Space Tech employees, their families and invited guests.

It didn't take a genius to know she was in the wrong place at the wrong time to pant after Brett like a lovesick puppy. If she could remember just ten good reasons why involvement with Brett was a bad idea, she'd be able to wrench her eyes away from his broad shoulders and slim hips. Ten more, and she'd forget how safe and protected she felt in his arms. One or two after that, and she might not recall every small kindness he had showered upon her, or the way his eyes sparkled whenever she walked into a room.

Her thoughts slowed. Time and reasoning would never help her forget. Seeing Brett Lincoln would always shatter the barriers she had constructed around her broken heart.

She had to get away.

Okay, the move to Washington offered a lot more than she'd originally thought. She could live in the nation's capital, where the town's most famous Lincoln wouldn't make her heart ache. The transfer even came with a major promotion, one she'd spent years working toward.

So why had she turned it down again?

The answer was guiding his charges down the sidewalk. She closed her eyes so she wouldn't have to see him.

Sometimes, you simply didn't get what you wanted. This was one of those times.

"Stephanie."

The familiar voice slowed the wrecking ball that Brett had aimed at her heart. One look at Mary's concerned face and Stephanie did not even try to wave off her friend.

As a mother of twins, Mary had learned not to waste time or words. "I saw Brett. Are you okay? You didn't know he'd be here?"

Blindly Stephanie shook her head. Because her ex-boyfriend was Tom's best friend, she and Mary made a point of steering their frequent conversations around Brett, but having this little piece of info up front would have been nice. The way it was, the advantage was all his.

"Oh, honey, I'm so sorry," Mary said when she did not answer. "I thought you knew. He's been working with PAL for weeks."

"Don't worry." Stephanie straightened her shoulders and firmed her flagging resolutions enough to reassure Mary, if not herself. "With this turnout, I can avoid him and the rest of the PAL contingent for one afternoon."

Mary shook her head. "I don't know about that, Steph. Brett really cares for those boys. Takes them fishing and to all sorts of things. I think you'll see a lot more of those three today."

That didn't sound like the Brett she knew.

Her breath tight within her chest, Stephanie turned toward the food pavilion where she expected Brett to dump the boys so he and his other buddies from the Police Athletic League could hang out together. Instead, the man of her dreams shadowed Jimmy and Joey's every step. Ignoring the group of chaperones gathered at the picnic tables, he shepherded the brothers through the food lines. After Mary returned to her own family, Stephanie watched him lead the way to the games. When she collected tickets at the moon bounce, Brett was right there, daring a reluctant Joey into gleeful handsprings while teasing smiles from his older brother. Throughout the day, he never strayed from their sides, or drifted from her thoughts. Until, by the time Ralinda paged her to the pavilion, Stephanie had reached the unmistakable conclusion that she'd been wrong.

Everything had changed.

THEY SAT shoulder to shoulder on folding chairs under the split-cedar shingles of the big pavilion with Brett's two charges on one side and Tom's family spread out on the other. Brett folded his copy of the schedule of events into quarters, and then into eighths. The agenda called for Stephanie to give the farewell speech—her farewell speech—before she cut the ribbon to let everyone into the big tent for the ice cream sundae feast. After that came the fishing derby, and then the day would finally be over. He could hold it together till then. The boys deserved that much.

"We have to sit through a speech before we get some ice cream. And we have to listen politely and clap at the end of it." Even if every word twisted the knife in his gut. "Okay, guys?"

"Who's gonna talk?" Jimmy demanded.

"Ms. Bryant. You met her at the bus." He thought he had been psyched up for the meeting, but one glimpse of Stephanie had ripped his wounded heart wide open.

"That pretty lady with her hair pulled back?" asked the younger brother.

Pretty wasn't the word for it. Even dressed in a loose T-shirt and a pair of long shorts, she still sent his pulse into overdrive. As for that ponytail, his fingers ached to free her hair and shake out the curls she had tamed and smoothed. "That's the one."

"I like her. She's nice," pronounced a yawning Joey. Four hours of bumper cars, the moon bounce and the trampoline, plus three-legged races and countless carnival games had tired the little guy. Brett pulled him close. An infusion of sugar, and the kid would be right back in the thick of things. He'd have to watch him like a daddy eagle then.

"I like her, too, buddy," he said, ruffling the boy's hair. "But she's giving a speech, and then she's moving far away."

"My daddy went far away. He's in heaven."

Joey's remark earned a derisive snort from his big brother, but Brett saw hurt burn in the hooded eyes. Moments later, the younger boy's eyelids drifted closed and his chin sank to his chest. Brett draped an arm around him, a motion that caught the twins' attention.

Barbara scrambled out of her seat and onto Brett's lap, framing his face with her two little hands. "No, Unca Brett. No boys," she whispered sternly.

It was all Brett could do not to laugh. "It's okay, sweetie," he said. He shifted Joey enough to make room for both girls. "See? Plenty of room. For boys and girls."

Barbara gave him a dubious look before snuggling into his arms without, he noticed, touching Joey. Brenda had other ideas.

"Miss Steppy, too," she demanded.

Knowing the little girl didn't really mean to plunge the knife so deep, Brett let out a long slow breath. "No, honey." He softened his tone. "Not Miss Steppy."

Gentle words or not, Brenda's lower lip began to tremble. The motion was a sure sign of impending tears, and Brett didn't try to stop her when she clambered to the floor and back to her mother's arms. She buried her head in Mary's embrace, refusing to glance in her traitorous uncle's direction. Brett swallowed a few tears of his own and hugged Barbara closer until a burst of applause drowned the roar of the surf.

Ten rows in front of them, Stephanie stepped onto center stage.

Here we go. Brett stiffened his shoulders and tightened his stomach.

When she tapped the mike, waited out the last splatters of applause and promised to keep her remarks short, he hoped she was lying because the longer she spoke, the longer she'd be around. Wondering if anyone else would miss her when she was gone, he spared a quick look at the gathered faces. The smiles told him that the head of human resources had endeared herself to her employees during her short tenure. How, then, could they let her go?

How could he? He had stared down the barrel of a gun without flinching, but the thought of losing Stephanie forever made him shake like a palm tree in a hurricane.

With a start, he realized he'd been drifting and she had come to the heart of her speech. He eased his chair back on two legs and braced himself.

"And now, I have some good news and some bad news. At least, it's good news for our D.C. office."

If they were at a wedding, this was the point where the minister would ask if anyone objected. *And I'd be on my feet shouting,* thought Brett. He no longer bothered trying to figure out why his thoughts turned to weddings whenever Stephanie was in the vicinity. The answer seemed all too obvious.

"Everyone knows John Sanders. Stand up, John."

Brett's forehead knotted as a man with glowing white

hair and a patrician face surged to his feet with the help of a cane. He gave a slight bow.

"Many of you know that John lives right here in Brevard County and, even though he retired a few years ago, he has remained an integral part of the Space Tech family. So much so that we've persuaded him to come out of retirement."

While everyone else applauded the good news, Brett ground his teeth. He was pretty sure the old guy was going to step into Stephanie's job so she could leave for Washington.

"What's the bad news, you ask?" Stephanie paused until she regained everyone's attention. "John has agreed to take on one of Space Tech's biggest challenges. He'll be moving to our nation's capital where he'll direct all of our efforts to become the country's number one supplier of advanced communications and networking solutions. I hope you'll join me in wishing good luck and a fond farewell to the man we all consider our close friend."

She. Wasn't. Leaving.

"Be cool," Brett breathed. Wanting to bolt out of his chair, rush through the crowd and demand answers, he waited until Stephanie finished before the front legs of his chair hit the floor. "Be cool."

Cool. He could do that. In spite of the flickering hope that threatened to turn into a raging wildfire, he could be totally cool. In fact, he was the picture of coolness.

He shifted Barbara to Tom's lap, shot his friend an offhand look and, in return, got a hearty clap on the back.

"I've got the boys," Tom said. "We'll get ice cream. You go get *her.*"

Brett was determined to do just that. Scattering apologies, he wove through the crowd that surged toward the ice cream tent until he reached the spot where he had last seen

Stephanie. True, he faced an uncool moment when he couldn't immediately find her, but the feeling quickly passed. The woman who haunted his dreams and was never far from his thoughts leaned against one of the wooden supports for the pavilion's vaulted ceiling.

Brett's feet slowed. He thirsted for a long look at her the way a man in the desert thirsted for water. When he realized she hadn't spotted him, he eased to one side and drank his fill.

Gone were the designer duds and strappy heels that revved his motor. She'd replaced them with off-the-rack Bermudas and a blousy Space Tech T-shirt that let her blend into the crowd and hid how special she was. Despite the casual get-up, Brett thought she looked sexier than ever. He swallowed and let his eyes roam where they wanted. They sought a pair of big blues that had once looked at him so tenderly. Behind them, he knew, lay fierce independence and the intelligence and determination to get what she wanted. She could go anywhere, have anything, including Space Tech's highest position. So why had she turned away from the very opportunity that had brought her to Florida and into his life?

Would she tell him? He looked expectantly at her pert lips. Recalling the feel of them pressed against his own, her mouth opening to him, the dance of her small tongue with his, he wondered if they could ever again have what they'd lost.

Stephanie.

Her name whispered through him. He wanted the whole package—love, marriage, a family of their own. He'd do whatever it took to make that happen, grovel if he had to. Anything to hold her in his arms and earn a second chance.

Whoa, big guy. Be cool, reminded his inner voice.

Brett nodded. He flexed his fingers while he practiced

the deep breathing he used on the gun range. Aiming for calm, he settled for marginally looser than hair-trigger tight. Any more deep breaths than that, and he was likely to hyperventilate. As it was, the ten steps to her side were the longest strides of his life.

"We need to talk," he announced. He missed his coolest voice by a couple of octaves, but it was close enough. "Why didn't you tell me you were staying?"

She spun toward him, a flare of hope showing in her eyes before protective armor dropped into place to hide it. Her arms crossed and she seemed to sink into the pillar, but her eyes did not waver as she faced him.

"What gave you the idea I was leaving?"

"Your sec—" Not wanting to cause any trouble, he started over. "I stopped by your office a couple of weeks ago. While I was there, I heard a rumor—"

"Oh? No one mentioned—"

She left the sentence unfinished, steering the conversation away from a path that would sidetrack both of them.

"John offered me the D.C. position. I turned it down. Turns out I'm not as committed to becoming Space Tech's CEO as I thought I was."

"And you're not going back to Ohio?" he asked. He stilled, not daring to move until he had her answer.

"I like it here," she said. "I think I can build a good life here."

He propped his hands, shoulder-width apart, above her on the pillar. She could walk away at any minute, but his stance formed a protective cave that announced "Keep Out" to anyone who might interrupt.

"You think that life could include me?" he asked, barely able to get the words out. A sheen of tears quickly extinguished the tiny spark of warmth he saw in her eyes.

"No," she said simply.

Coolness was highly overrated. Someone who was truly cool would never ask the question that leaped from his lips.

"Why?"

He refused to look away, even as her words sliced through his heart.

"You're the reason I nearly accepted the transfer. Even though we've never said it, I know we love each other. But I need more than that. I need to be first in your life. I won't settle for anything less."

Brett felt the stirrings of an old prejudice and quashed them. Putting herself first didn't make Stephanie selfish or self-centered. It made her whole and independent. It was part of what he loved about her.

"You are the most important person in my life," he swore. "You have been since the day we met."

In his dreams, words like those led to kisses and warm embraces. Reality didn't bring the same results. Stephanie's arms remained firmly crossed.

"Oh?"

Who knew one word could hold so much challenge?

"If that's true, why did we break up? What happened to us, Brett?"

"I forgot to cancel our date." The reason sounded as trivial as he always thought it would, but it was the only one he had. Evidently, there was more because Stephanie waited for him to add something, something that was beyond his grasp. He floundered, unable to find it.

"That's why we fought," she said at last. "That's *not* why we broke up. We stopped seeing each other because…" She drew in a breath so deep it seemed to shudder all the way up from her toes. "Remember the day Pat's Place was robbed?"

"Remember? How could I forget the day you called it quits?"

He stared at the tears trailing down her cheeks. It didn't matter that he hadn't meant to do it, he'd wounded her. Insight tugged at his consciousness and made him shake his head like a gator trout throwing a hook. He had to tell her he was trying.

"I've changed a lot since then. I took your advice—all of it. I do volunteer work now. Exercise. I gave up the bar scene." The recitation sounded too much like a job application. He stopped himself. "It'll take some time, but you'll see."

"But that day," she breathed. "You stood me up to be with your friends. You didn't even tell me…"

The confusion he felt spilled into his voice. "I didn't tell you…what?"

"You didn't tell me you faced down an armed suspect in a robbery. Why didn't you tell me how close I came to losing you? You told everyone…"

She waited a beat while Brett's heart skipped several. "…but me."

As if it had taken all she had to get the words out, she slumped against the pillar. Her cheeks glistened wetly, and she refused to meet his eyes.

He had picked up the phone a dozen times that day, but he had never placed the one call that mattered. Now, nothing mattered more than making things right between them. He only knew one way to do that. He prayed it would be enough.

"Stephanie, honey, I'm sorry. I am so sorry. Except to tell Jake to stop harassing you, I haven't hung with the guys since that night. I don't need anyone else in my life. You. You're all I need. All I ever wanted."

She raised her face until her wide blue eyes met his. Hope shot through him at the possibility he saw shimmering through her tears. Uncertain whether he could believe it or not, he hesitated. "Stephanie? Honey? Will you give me another chance?"

Her lips curved up in a tentative smile that hinted at a future of possibilities.

"Maybe," she whispered. "If you stop calling me *honey*."

It was such a small thing to give up.

"The word will never cross my lips again," he vowed. And this time, he meant it.

STARING UP AT HIM, Stephanie knew that no matter how much he looked like one, Brett was not a god—Greek or otherwise. He was a man, with all the foibles that made him who he was…and she loved him with all her heart. So what if he was so sure of himself it drove her mad? She wouldn't love him half as much if he were any different. Besides, she also knew that beneath Brett's proud exterior beat a heart soft enough to admit when he was wrong.

They could build a life with that.

The realization of how close they'd come to losing each other propelled her straight into his outstretched arms.

"I was so scared that I'd lost you," she whispered. She stood on tiptoe to search his face. "Don't ever scare me like that again."

"Never," he swore without hesitation.

One word. Despite the summerlike heat, she'd been cold ever since the day they'd called it quits. Yet with that one word, he had chased away the chill.

Brett brushed his lips against her hair. "I'll do anything to keep you. Anything at all. Ask me something I can promise."

She knew just the thing. Stephanie pressed close enough to feel the way his heart pounded in his broad chest. "Will you stay with me?" she asked.

"Forever," he murmured as she clung to his solid strength. "I've got you forever."

Though she felt safe in his arms, she had to be sure. "And you love me? The way I love you?"

"With all my life." A fire that matched her own blazed in his eyes. Swearing he'd never let go, he bent down.

Anticipation built to a fever pitch within her and Stephanie rose to meet Brett halfway. Full of promise, his lips brushed hers. He tasted of salt and cola, and she opened to him, eager to immerse herself in his kisses and follow wherever that led.

Behind them, someone coughed.

Brett stilled. His blue eyes peered down at her. "Why do I have the feeling we've got an audience?" he muttered.

Stephanie stole a quick look past his shoulder. Sure enough, Tom stood a not-so-discreet five feet away with the twins, Brett's little guys and Mary crowded behind him.

"Sorry to interrupt, you two," Tom said with a smug grin. "It's time for the fishing derby."

"Already?" Brett grumbled. He leaned close enough that his breath sent shivers of pleasure rippling through her. "We were just getting started," he whispered.

Stephanie smiled up at the face she would never tire of seeing. At their first opportunity, they'd pick up their interrupted kiss where they'd left off, but for now, they both had obligations to fulfill.

"Looks like we'll have to finish this later. Think you can handle that?" she asked. Her heart raced at the way his eyes smoldered, promising more. Raining kisses on her cheeks and nose, Brett pulled back.

"I can handle anything with you beside me." He pressed her close to his side and swung them around to face the others.

Tom aimed a thumb toward Mary and the children. "The girls are eager to fish with their Unca Brett. So are the boys. Are you ready for this?"

"I am now," Brett answered. He aimed an elbow in Tom's direction while his arm at her waist tightened enough to let Stephanie know he intended to keep her close. "Ready, girls? Ready, boys?" he called to the children.

"Ready," four voices chorused in unison.

"Then let's go catch us a marlin," he dared.

Brett's touch skimmed from her waist to her fingertips. Folding her hand in his, he led them toward the fishing pier and their future. As they stepped from beneath the shaded pavilion, Stephanie checked the sky for storm clouds, a habit she'd developed since moving to Florida. It looked as if the weatherman had miscalculated again—there was no sign of the predicted thunderstorms. From where she stood, clear skies and bright sunshine stretched all the way to the end of the ocean.

* * * * *

*Harlequin Intrigue top author Delores Fossen
presents a brand-new series of
breathtaking romantic suspense!*
TEXAS MATERNITY: HOSTAGES
The first installment available May 2010:
THE BABY'S GUARDIAN

Shaw cursed and hooked his arm around Sabrina.

Despite the urgency that the deadly gunfire created, he tried to be careful with her, and he took the brunt of the fall when he pulled her to the ground. His shoulder hit hard, but he held on tight to his gun so that it wouldn't be jarred from his hand.

Shaw didn't stop there. He crawled over Sabrina, sheltering her pregnant belly with his body, and he came up ready to return fire.

This was obviously a situation he'd wanted to avoid at all cost. He didn't want his baby in the middle of a fight with these armed fugitives, but when they fired that shot, they'd left him no choice. Now, the trick was to get Sabrina safely out of there.

"Get down," someone on the SWAT team yelled from the roof of the adjacent building.

Shaw did. He dropped lower, covering Sabrina as best he could.

There was another shot, but this one came from a rifleman on the SWAT team. Shaw didn't look up, but he heard the sound of glass being blown apart.

The shots continued, all coming from his men, which

meant it might be time to try to get Sabrina to better cover. Shaw glanced at the front of the building.

So that Sabrina's pregnant belly wouldn't be smashed against the ground, Shaw eased off her and moved her to a sitting position so that her back was against the brick wall. They were close. Too close. And face-to-face.

He found himself staring right into those sea-green eyes.

How will Shaw get Sabrina out?
Follow the daring rescue and the heartbreaking
aftermath in THE BABY'S GUARDIAN
by Delores Fossen,
available May 2010 from Harlequin Intrigue.

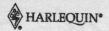

Bestselling Harlequin Presents® author

Lynne Graham

introduces

VIRGIN ON HER
WEDDING NIGHT

Valente Lorenzatto never forgave Caroline Hales's
abandonment of him at the altar. But now he's
made millions and claimed his aristocratic Venetian
birthright—and he's poised to get his revenge.
He'll ruin Caroline's family by buying out their
company and throwing them out of their mansion…
unless she agrees to give him the wedding night
she denied him five years ago.…

**Available May 2010
from Harlequin Presents!**

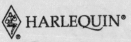

HARLEQUIN®

LAURA MARIE ALTOM

The Baby Twins

Stephanie Olmstead has her hands full raising
her twin baby girls on her own. When she runs
into old friend Brady Flynn, she's shocked to find
herself suddenly attracted to the handsome airline
pilot! Will this flyboy be the perfect daddy—
or will he crash and burn?

"LOVE, HOME & HAPPINESS"

www.eHarlequin.com

HAR

Former bad boy Sloan Hawkins is back in
Redemption, Oklahoma, to help keep his aunt's
cherished garden thriving and to reconnect with the
girl he left behind, Annie Markham. But when he
discovers his secret child—and that single mother
Annie never stopped loving him—he's determined
that a wedding will take place in the garden
nurtured by faith and love.

REDEMPTION
RIVER

Where healing flows...

Look for

The Wedding Garden
by Linda Goodnight

Available May 2010
wherever you buy books.

REQUEST YOUR FREE BOOKS!
2 FREE NOVELS PLUS 2 FREE GIFTS!

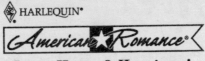

HARLEQUIN®

American ★ Romance®

Love, Home & Happiness!